FAKE IT SO REAL

SUSAN SANFORD BLADES

NIGHTWOOD EDITIONS

2020

Nightwood Editions
P.O. Box 1779
Gibsons, BC VON 1V0
Canada
www.nightwoodeditions.com

COVER DESIGN: Angela Yen
COVER ILLUSTRATION: Robert Charleton
TYPOGRAPHY: Shed Simas/Onça Design

Nightwood Editions acknowledges the support of the Canada Council for the Arts, the Government of Canada, and the Province of British Columbia through the BC Arts Council.

This book has been produced on 100% post-consumer recycled, ancient-forest-free paper, processed chlorine-free and printed with vegetable-based dyes.

Printed and bound in Canada.

LIBRARY AND ARCHIVES CANADA CATALOGUING IN PUBLICATION
Title: Fake it so real / by Susan Sanford Blades.
Names: Sanford Blades, Susan, author.
Identifiers: Canadiana (print) 20200213652 | Canadiana (ebook) 20200213660 | ISBN 9780889713888 (softcover) | ISBN 9780889713895 (ebook)
Classification: LCC PS8637.A56 F35 2020 | DDC C813/.6—dc23

Contents

For Benji, Simeon and Noam

Poseurs

Shepps entered Gwen's life through the seagull shit–streaked doors of Pluto's Diner one hot Monday in June of 1983. Braceleted by masking tape, bowed by duffle bag, he was as greasy and limp as an undercooked french fry. He pulled a poster from his bag and asked Gwen if she could spare a bit of wall for his band. It was five minutes 'til close. Gwen had been traipsing around the joint, braless in a pit-stained T-shirt, snarling at customers through her ever-moist Fire Red pout, losing pens in her bleached-blonde witch's broom for the past eight hours. She flumped her torso over the counter and reached for the sheet Shepps offered.

Lock the door, wouldja? she said. Dorothy's Rainbow?

At the OAP Hall Friday.

I'm going to that show. To see the Neos.

Red Tide's playing too.

Too surfy for me. I like it harder. What are you, Raffi? Fred Penner? Singalongs?

Punk rock.

Name isn't punk.

Wasn't my idea.

But it's your band?

Shepps lowered his head and rifled through his bag for an explanation. Gwen had a nose for liars. This guy couldn't command a sentence, let alone a stage. She pegged him as a wrist-stamper, a hanger-on, occasional tambourine shaker.

We were going to be ska, Shepps said, but my bassist thought punk would get us more chicks.

Does it?

Does for Donny. My bassist. Dude looks like Sid Vicious. Ferries to Seattle every few weeks to give blood for a living and eats nothing but Twizzlers and pussy. Even has track marks.

Hot.

Shepps perched himself on a stool across from Gwen. He was thin as a willow switch, draped in a neon-splattered cotton tee. This guy didn't give a shit, but in a clueless ten-year-old-boy way.

What's your poison? Gwen said, and before he could answer she poured him a glass of apple juice. She poured herself a vodka and let him lie to her. He told her he dug the band but wanted to quit. He bemoaned his toad voice. The girls. Every night like a lineup for the dole outside his van—myriad desperate faces with ready palms. Shepps' lies endeared him to Gwen. This one lied due to the unbearableness of the truth. Nights spent jacking off in a sleeping bag with a broken zipper, judged by the blinking silver eyes of his tambourine. Days spent pointlessly sticking paper to walls, begging the band for a larger role—backup vocals, cowbell. Gwen let him eat her out atop the counter after close, his lips sticky from the apple juice. When she came he leaned his head on her slick thigh and said, You're delicious.

Is it really your band?

I play bass.

What about Donny?

I play second bass.

Is that necessary?

Not fresh-air necessary.

Every afternoon that week at five minutes 'til close, in traipsed Shepps like a lost puppy. He'd clunk his elbows to the counter, smush his cheeks into his fists, and sheepishly order an apple juice. When he slurped his cup dry he tapped Gwen's wrist and said, May I eat you out now? Shepps smeared Gwen over every inch of vinyl in the place. Gwen's boss pulled her into a booth one morning and said, Smell the bench, Gwen. What is that? Bleach? Pancake batter? She dipped her nostrils, shrugged and told him the cook closed the night before.

By Thursday, Gwen hated the way Shepps stared at her through his strands of oiled mullet. With every reverent look, she felt less vindicated in her foul manner, less herself. She hated the way he wriggled his lips around his straw, like an elephant grasping at a peanut. She hated the way he wore his threadbare ripped jeans slung low, teetered between his hips, with no visible bunch of boxer above the waistline. That he allowed his penis free rein between his thighs like a medal she wasn't privy to. She hated that he never removed his pants, that this was all about her pleasure, his tongue, his fingers. She hated the regularity of his visits. She hated that she anticipated them. And when he didn't show up that Friday, she hated *him*.

Friday night, Gwen attended the OAP show flanked by her roommates Mona and Christie. She wanted Shepps to see her, but to not see her seeing him. Mona blew Hubba bubbles and yelled menstrual anxieties into Gwen's ear. Can you tell I'm wearing a pad? Is there blood showing? I felt a gush. Christie, a Bryan Adams fan, stayed only for Donny, in his *Tofino Has Crabs* T-shirt and egg white-firm mohawk. She angled herself toward his low-vibrating corner of the stage and gathered all available armpit flesh into the underwire of her bra to create maximum cleavage. Every time Donny tossed his chin toward the crowd, she yanked Gwen's elbow and whispered, Jesus.

Shepps stood sandwiched between Donny and the drum kit. He wore a blond ringleted wig and tight jeans with an embellished crotch—an allusion to Robert Plant that only accentuated his dissimilarity to the Golden God.

The real leader of the band was Damian Costello. He was not 1983 beautiful. His hair had not made the acquaintance of clippers. His testicles had not been heated to the point of sterility by a pair of tight, acid-washed jeans. His beauty transcended decades. God, how he moved. Skinny and lithe as a garden hose. Johnny Rotten's death grip on the mic stand without the toothy maw.

After the show, Shepps sidled up to Gwen and invited her and her friends to an after-party in his home—an orange Westfalia he parked at Clover Point. She nodded, eyes fixed on Damian, and despite herself, followed the band. Christie climbed to the Westie's pop top and dangled a bare leg over the edge at Donny. He took the bait and, seconds later, her bra parachuted to the floor while she produced that second-base gargled moan that encouraged guys to slide into third. The drummer, Ricky, supplied the band with weed, a steady beat, and a throaty guffaw from time to time, but spoke little and the girls therefore considered him sexless. Damian listlessly twanged Mona's bra strap then excused himself to get some air. Gwen had avoided Shepps all night, kept her head turned at a forty-five degree angle from him, offering only her left ear.

He mumbled into that ear, May I—

Keep Mona company, Gwen said. You can finger her a bit, I won't mind.

Where are you going?

Gwen opened the sliding door. Mona, I've told you about Shepps, right?

Sure, Mona said. Inarticulate, likes to eat pussy?

Gwen slammed the door and spotted Damian, out to sea, knee-deep in kelp. She plunged toward him like a spoon through Jell-O and said, Howdy, then wished she'd opened with something more punk rock like *Oi!*, then realized that was too effortful and *Howdy* was so unpunk rock that it, in fact, was punk rock and felt satisfied with herself.

How'd you like the show? Damian didn't remove his attention from the Olympic range.

The Neos rocked. Red Tide, meh. You sucked.

He spun to face Gwen. Yeah? He tucked a few strands of hair behind his ear and lifted his lips to the left like his face was half frozen.

Yeah. "God Save Pierre Elliott Trudeau"? What is that?

My dad pays for my loft in Chinatown. How about you?

My parents disowned me when I bleached my hair. Gwen scratched her scalp. They still pay my rent.

All those kids at the show—those Oak Bay kids—their moms wipe their asses with hundred dollar bills. And we're no different. We're privileged Canadians. Toying with anger. We're not punk rock.

Dayglos are punk rock.

The Dayglo Abortions are legit badass. So punk they don't call themselves punk.

I know, Gwen said, then wondered if it might be more punk rock to admit to not know what she pretended to know.

Damian yoinked a sea-salted strand of Gwen's hair. Why look like Nancy Spungen? She was psychotic.

Would you prefer Nancy Sinatra?

Psychotic's good. Damian lifted Gwen and splashed and stumbled and shimmied her onto the beach and banged her head on a rock before flopping on top of her. She let him fuck her like a man who, after a day inking paper, had returned home to his aproned wife and slipper-bearing dog, meat loaf firming in the oven. She let him come in five minutes, tuck his limp sea cucumber into his pants, and saunter back to the van because Gwen was twenty-one years old and beautiful boys didn't need to try.

That July, Damian's coffee table supported five bags of Cheetos, an ashtray, Gwen's bare ass, two guitars, seven pipes, Ricky's spare change, Damian's bare ass, the soles of Gwen's shit-kickers, one issue of *Verbal Assault*, seven tea lights, ten two-sixes of vodka, one burning stick of patchouli, three boogers, one wad of Hubba Bubba and a small, terrifying object.

Gwen pointed to the urine-soaked blue line and said, Do we want this?

Damian bent his head over his guitar, face shrouded by hair, noodled a tune, then peered over the sides of his knees toward the coffee table. Has it been long enough?

The line doesn't disappear with time.

Baybeh, sang Damian, and Gwen wasn't sure whether it was a noodling emission or a proclamation of their future.

So?

Do we want a baybeh, sang Damian. He looked up now, not at Gwen, but beyond her, eyes dim and glazed as though scanning a crowd for the hottest, most vulnerable-looking blonde.

So, no?

Do we want to kill a baybeh.

I don't think I do.

Me neither.

Which one?

The killing one.

Damian put down his guitar. Gwen watched him pull up his saggy socks. Did Johnny Rotten wear socks, and if so, were they from the sale bin at Canadian Tire, greyish white with the elastic gone?

Damian picked up the test. Fuck, yeah. A baby. An experiment. A tiny me. He waved the test around like a conductor's baton.

It's not in the stick. Gwen raised her eyebrows and pointed to her stomach.

He tossed the stick onto the coffee table and clenched a fistful of Gwen's shirt. We'll get married, he said.

Gwen smiled. She wrapped her hands around his fist.

We won't tell anyone.

Gwen frowned and dropped her hands.

Except Shepps. He'll be the ring bearer.

We'll make him wear a dress.

Sad little flower girl.

Shepps did not wear a dress but he grasped the flowers like a little girl. He brought them himself—lavender and daisies he'd picked on the way to City Hall. They flopped over the side of his fist as though ambling to the tune of his daydreams. I love lavender, Gwen said. Shepps said, I know. Gwen squeezed his free hand. It was clammy, childlike. Damian's hands were dry as sandpaper, inhuman. We've never talked about lavender, Gwen said, and followed Damian into City Hall.

Gwen wore her grade twelve graduation dress—a fuchsia, puff-sleeved, polka-dotted number—because punk rock would soon die but polka dots were forever. Damian wore something Gwen had never seen—low-slung bell-bottoms he'd rolled up tight to conceal their outdated girth and a black suit jacket sized for a child. He looked like a lanky giant dragging two lumpy doughnuts at his ankles. Gwen was about to marry someone whose full spectrum of pants she was not yet acquainted with.

Gwen had not been the sort of little girl who enacted a white wedding with a dandelion tied around her finger and her boy-neighbour's ketchup chip–powdered lips thrust against her cheek. She spent the idle summer days of her childhood melting her dolls' plastic faces with a magnifying glass and dodging said boy-neighbour's arc of urine through the gaps in their shared fence. She was at City Hall to sing the anthem of The Man because Damian was there too and she could not say no to the one person who could say no to her.

Their wedding subverted all weddings. The marriage commissioner wore sweatpants, pilled and thin at the rear. He scratched at his crotch and Gwen was not positive he'd put on underwear. With each question, he glanced at the clock and tamped his growling stomach with a flat palm. Sorry, he said, I haven't taken lunch. Shepps scattered the lavender at his feet and patted himself in search of gum. Damian offered the commissioner a peanut found in his pocket and he paused the ceremony to crack the shell, chew at the two little legumes and scratch a finger at the bits of thin, rusted skin that clung to his incisors. When the commissioner asked Damian if he undertook to afford Gwen the love of his person etcetera, instead of saying I do, Damian replied: Fuck yeah. And when he signed the registration of marriage, his signature was different from that on his rent cheques. It was lazy, scrawled, defiant. Was he sticking it to The Man or to Gwen?

After the ceremony, Shepps took Gwen and Damian to Pluto's for a milkshake. Gwen hadn't seen Shepps in Pluto's since he'd last kneeled before a booth, clamped between her knees. He ordered two milkshakes and an apple juice. Gwen faced the two men across the table from her in silence. She hadn't had a conversation of note with either of the two in the few months she'd known them. Shepps was more familiar with her vulva than her mouth. Neither of them knew her favourite colour, though both were impressed with her affinity for the Slits. Gwen scowled into her milkshake, counted the seconds her straw could remain independently erect.

Shepps raised his glass and said, Congrats Dams. His voice trailed off and he bit his lips together as his mouth curved up, retaining his guilty anticipation of the spoils of this union.

Damian tilted his head toward Shepps and rolled his straw between his molars. I feel like we just robbed a bank, he said.

Gwen lifted her straw and sucked a glob of milkshake off the end. What now? she said.

Shepps shuffled into the postnatal ward of the Royal Jubilee Hospital the day after Sara Rae Costello was born. He had always been loose-gaited, but that day he seemed invertebrate. Gwen was without company, baby or makeup.

You had a baby. It was the most punk rock thing Shepps had ever said.

Long time no see, Shepps.

Where's Dams?

He cut the cord and fucked off.

How's married life?

The masochist in me loves it.

Shepps smiled and looked at Gwen as if to say *You're delicious,* but instead he said, You're tired. Gwen asked him how he was and he said he was good in a sleepy, elastic tone that made her hate him and everyone who had a life outside her hospital bed. They sat and looked at the walls until a nurse brought in the baby.

Shepps said, She's beautiful. You look beautiful holding a baby. You look beautiful feeding a baby. And they looked at the baby until he said, I should go.

You don't have to, Gwen said.

You should rest.

Gwen held her free hand out to him and he filled it with a bouquet of lavender he'd squished into his coat pocket.

I love lavender, she said, but Shepps had already slumped out, led by his forehead and toes.

Sara had a sly smile Gwen loathed, the same smile Damian formed when conjuring alibis. After three years of marriage, Gwen's nose was full of lies. Sara reserved her smile for moments of mischief. Cheerio-paste paintings on the carpet, feces on the bathroom wall. She sensed Gwen's frustration and up those lips curled, followed by a plea for Daddy. Daddy received genuine smiles. Giggles, even. Sara bestowed a jowly, Churchillian frown on Gwen.

Gwen dreaded the times Sara was not unconscious. Dread of building blocks, tea parties, the inescapable child's gaze. Dread of mistakes. Every motion, emotion, utterance potentially lethal. This child weighed too much. At times, she would offer Gwen respite. She'd run a peanut-buttered finger through Gwen's tangled hair, allow Gwen's lips to reach the crown of her head, succumb to sleep on Gwen's downy stomach.

Gwen never felt so observed as when she took Sara out of the apartment. White-haired women fitted in tweed and leather gawked and remarked on the uncomfortable tilt of Sara's napping head or the discrepancy between the day's wind speed and the girl's bare feet. Gwen visited playgroups in search of camaraderie. She was a fuck-up among the blushed and shoulder-padded Oak Bay moms who spoke of carpet swatches, gated tropical vacation rentals and their husbands' stock portfolios. She was a goody-goody among the spiked and acned Fernwood teen pregnancy crew who penciled math homework on vomit-crinkled loose-leaf and spoke of upcoming beach fires and not husbands or even boyfriends, but baby-daddies and dealers.

Gwen scorned and admired them all. She wanted to extract cross-sections of each of them—this one's ability to change a diaper on a gymnasium floor with a stray sock, a safety pin and a muffin wrapper dipped in coffee dregs; that one's cockleshell lips the light-pink hue of haphazard chapping and kissing—and create an ally, a friend, a community. But she remained catatonic on benches against walls, opening her mouth only to correct Sara's social blunders.

Damian had no trouble with the girl. Parenting is simpler for the absent. When home, Damian puddled himself over the living room couch, a foundation upon which Sara enacted her day. Last night's shirt on his back became her doll's sleeping bag; his pockets, containers for her snacks of marshmallows and chocolate chips. He would join her games as a beached merman or chicken pox victim, nothing that required a plumb spine. Words that were meaningless from Gwen's lips—words like *enough*, *now*, *because*—were respected commands from Damian. Gwen understood. She also celebrated the reprieves from Damian's quiet disinterest.

One July night, after Sara's limbs had softened to curlicues around afghans, bears and mythical creatures, Gwen leaned over her balcony rail like a child in line for a carnival ride, and watched passersby. She was glad she wasn't them. They were old and crippled. Saddled with groceries and offspring. Fashion victims. Having obvious, pretend fun. Slumping along, zombie-like, as though every crack in the sidewalk were an abyss to traverse.

Gwen yelled, Not playing tonight?

Shepps swayed like a poplar in the breeze. Gwen? He cupped his eyes with his hands and looked up at her. Gwen hadn't seen Shepps in years. She patted her hair, now long and unbleached, squirrel brown. She held her hands to cover the overripe plum napping under each eye.

Why aren't you playing tonight? she repeated.

No show tonight.

Then where's Damian? Gwen dangled her arms over the railing. Why don't I ever see you?

You don't come to our gigs.

I'm under house arrest.

Finally caught you?

Why don't you come up? Gwen's fingers grasped at the air as though to bail out the sky between them.

Maybe for a minute, Shepps said.

Five minutes, Gwen said. Come in. Talk to me. Lie with me.

Shepps lay with Gwen in her bed, an inert palm to her hip. He told her the truth about his new job pumping at the Esso. She smelled his sweet and sour fingers. He told her about quitting the band. I don't know if they need two bassists, he said.

Then Shepps lied to her about a girl. Cindy or Sandy or Mindy who worked the coffee stand at the Esso. Filled her uniform well. Snug, he said. She'd been to his van for a beer. He'd undone a few of her buttons, and then a few more. He might take her up island, introduce her to surfing, black bears, his parents.

You don't even have parents, Gwen said. She pressed her palm to his hand on her hip. Gwen thought about his sickly sweet tongue. How disposable it once was. And how much depended on it now.

Sock Daddy

Gwen's daughters found their father's sock the spring after he left, when the nights grew short and the plums grew blossoms. Gwen had been in bed so long it seemed pointless to get out. The girls tumbled over one another around its outskirts in a slithery game of leapfrog. The eldest, Sara, shrieked and giggled, and her baby sister Meg ribbited. Their stubby fingers grasped at the sheets to avoid hardwood-smacked tailbones and closet door handle–driven skulls. Gwen's limp body swayed like seaweed with each tug from either side of the bed. Then the little fingers released the sheet and there was an audible pause before the girls began to whisper, sinister and insistent. Gwen rolled over to see Sara's hand encased by a thin, white tube sock, a trail of dust draped from its toe bed like a princess's ribbon. Sara raised a bony, freckled arm above her head.

I found Daddy, she said.

The sock had lived under Gwen's bed, ensnared by a warren of dust bunnies, for months, since before Christmas when all was grey and damp. Since her husband's band played a gig in Vancouver. Since he called from a pay phone and remained silent when she'd said, *I want you to want to come home*. Since the band's van *put-put-putt*ed to a slump under her window and only the second bassist, Shepps, emerged—a messenger with body shrouded in baggy plaid, face shrouded in greased brown hair, designs on Gwen shrouded in sympathy.

When Shepps buzzed that night, Gwen's voice scratched through her apartment building's speaker, Where's Damian?

I don't know.

You don't know?

He took off. Said he'd meet us but didn't show.

You waited how long?

'Til the last ferry.

Why didn't you wait longer?

Will you let me up?

Gwen let Shepps in. She didn't need an answer. The band didn't wait longer for her husband for the same reason she wouldn't. Why expect someone to return to a home he'd never truly inhabited?

For a week, the sock dangled from Sara's hand, a droopy, browning ghost. It held her peanut butter sandwiches, her crayons, her toilet paper. It smacked her baby sister, it swam in the bath. When Gwen stumbled to Sara's room to tuck her in at night, she'd spy Sara in the glow of her night light with the sock held to her mouth. The sock consumed itself into her fist while she whispered to it.

Why didn't you come back, Daddy? Did you fall in the ocean? Did you join the mermen?

Gwen assumed Sara would lose interest in the sock. Sara constantly switched favourites with her dolls. A few months earlier, she had loved Maggie with her enviable Goldilocks hair and her comforting imperfections—the red smudge from her lip to her right dimple, the unravelled thread of her left knee. Then Sara's affections turned to Baby Betty, whose fluffy round head Sara would cup in her armpit. When Betty's fluff had worn, Sara prized Little Sara, whose hard plastic face made a tinging sound when bumped along the metal balusters of the building's stairs. But Sock Daddy had not left Sara's right hand for a full week.

Shepps and his van had haunted the street below Gwen's window since his return from Vancouver that December. When Gwen needed Cheetos, vodka or rent money, Shepps slept in her bed. When Gwen swore she saw him gawk from the balcony at a jogger's frenetic cleavage, when he breathed too loudly during *Baywatch* or ate the last Cheeto, he slept in his van.

At week two, a note accompanied Sara's bread crusts and the brown bits of apple she'd spat into her lunch kit. It was written in cursive on a cat-shaped Post-it note. *Can we talk about the sock?* The first word that came to Gwen's mind was: vague. Then: condescending. Then: who writes in cursive except grade one teachers? Then: well, she *is* a grade one teacher. Finally: fuck.

The next morning at seven a.m., Gwen looked out her window for Shepps' floppy form in the van below. His windows were fogged. Who else was in there? Probably that tramp who worked at the 7-Eleven, always sucking on sour candies. Shepps did not have the fortitude to fend off sexual advances borne by minimum-wage desperation and sugared blue tongues. Gwen reminded herself windows could also fog from one person breathing his own sullen van air.

Gwen pulled a boho skirt out of a box of old clothes in her closet. Its whimsical colour scheme would appeal to—or at least distract—a grade one teacher. The skirt last graced her form seven years ago, the summer she met Damian. When her lips were thick and red and had never uttered words like *betrayal* or *baby wipe*. But she could not force the skirt's gasping mouth to zip. Gwen settled for worn jeans, holed in unfashionable areas— hips, crotch, cuffs—and a crop top which, if she held her breath, was almost appropriate. This was how good mothers dressed. A good mother puts her children's needs above her own appearance.

Gwen and the girls paraded out of the apartment, their teeth gummed with cereal crumbs, their hands milk-sticky. Sara smeared the sock's wide-open jaw along the stairwell's peeling wallpaper. Once outside, Gwen smacked a palm to the window of Shepps' van and pressed the bridge of her nose to the glass. No sour-candy girl, only stretched-out Shepps, alone and there, always there. Shepps shifted and turned to face Gwen. She stepped back, guilty of voyeurism and care, and stumbled over Meg behind her.

Goddamnit, Meg. Always at my feet.

Shepps poked his head out the van's window. Where you going?

Sissy school, said Meg. She latched five chubby fingers onto Gwen's back pocket.

A bit early?

Meeting with the teacher. Gwen twitched her head toward Sara, who squirmed the sock into Meg's brown curls and made monsterly eating noises, *Ump. Ump. Ump.*

Shepps gave Gwen that look the bank teller gives when you're overdrawn. Smug pity.

Meg giggled and patted both palms atop her head in unison. Stop, Sock Daddy, stop.

Need a ride? Shepps rubbed his eyes.

We don't need anything.

Want a ride?

You should probably go back to sleep.

I'm offering, Gwen.

I don't need your pity.

It's not pity, it's a van.

We're fine, Gwen said.

Why can't we get a ride? Sock Daddy doesn't like walking. Sara tilted the sock's head downward. Her fingers had gathered its fabric into a tight-lipped pout with puffs of thinned, grey cheeks, where the pads of Damian's feet once roamed.

Sock Daddy can't always have what he wants, Gwen said.

Miss Howe sat in a miniature chair across from Gwen, who sat atop the "Explore and Discover" table beside a tub of dry rice. Meg lay sprawled face down on the classroom floor at Gwen's feet. She sealed her lips around a pile of pencil shavings and puffed her cheeks with air. Sara kneeled at Meg's head, growled and nipped at her with the sock.

Meg, gross, Gwen said.

Sara slid the sock under Meg's mouth and said, Meggie don't. It's germy.

It's quite natural for a child to form an attachment to an inanimate object, Miss Howe said. But lately Sara's been a little... Miss Howe held her open palm toward Sara.

Dog-like?

More like...

Violent?

Miss Howe turned her head away from where Sara and Meg pawed at one another on the floor. She opened her eyes wide and mouthed the word *nefarious*.

Fairyish?

Miss Howe cupped her hands, leaned toward Gwen, and repeated herself.

Gwen wiped the lipstick from her mouth with the back of her hand. Her father left us a few months ago. It's his sock, she said.

Miss Howe brought hand to heart.

I can't take it away from her.

Of course not.

She's got a grip on that thing.

Well, I wouldn't suggest...

What do you mean, *nefarious*?

Miss Howe tapped at her collarbone with the fingers of one hand, a fluttering half butterfly. Some of the children—

Meg yanked on the end of the sock. Sara raised the sock above Meg's head and hissed, then beaked at Meg's face with it like an angry, off-white goose. Meg held the backs of her hands to her face and swatted up a tornado of Sara's long brown hair with her palms.

Girls, Gwen shrieked, then continued in faux calm. That's not how we treat our sisters.

Does she do this at home? Miss Howe said.

Out the window, children congregated in maniacal ball-hurling, stick-wielding herds. Little stockbrokers in anticipation of their mayhem-cueing bell. Gwen didn't know if Sara did this at home. At home, Gwen lived from bubble bath to bed. Everything in between was a vodka-smeared blur.

He was in a punk band, Gwen said. They had this big gig in Vancouver and then he just...

Mmm hmm. Miss Howe nodded.

Stayed.

Miss Howe nodded.

There, I mean.

Do you have support?

Not here.

Anyone to help?

Not that he was ever around much anyway.

Your parents?

Gwen flapped her lips. My parents? Nope.

That man who brings Sara to and from school?

Shepps? He's the second bassist.

I'm sorry?

In the band.

Hmm? Oh the—Sara's father's.

Meg squeezed a bit of Gwen's jeans in each hand and pulled herself to her knees. Her floor-swirled curls carpeted Gwen's lap.

Gwen raked Meg's curls with her fingers. What about Shepps?

Miss Howe patted Meg's head. I want to ensure there's support for you and the girls.

He's around. For now.

Meg pulled at the neck of Gwen's shirt and climbed atop her lap. Sara slithered the sock up Gwen's leg like a boa constrictor. She lifted its mouth level with Gwen's face, opened her hand inside and whispered, Sock Daddy doesn't like you.

Gwen swatted at the sock. Stop it, Sara.

Sara turned the sock hand to face her own eyes and asked, Sock Daddy, why don't you like Mommy?

She's smelly, the sock told Sara in a gravelly voice.

Gwen stood and dropped Meg to her bottom on the floor. I'm done, she said. We're out. Have a good day at school, Sara.

She's smeeeeeeelly. Sara slid to her back on the floor. She waved the sock hand above her in a half windmill, a malevolent rhythmic gymnastics routine.

Gwen grabbed at Meg's hand, which she flopped out of reach.

She's smelly and she doesn't brush her teeth, the sock said to Miss Howe. Miss Howe reached toward the sock and it attempted to swallow her hand whole, boa constrictor style. Miss Howe tittered and pocketed her hand.

Get. Up. Meg. Now. Gwen pulled at Meg's wrist and dragged her by her diapered bottom out of the classroom and into the hall. Once away from adult supervision, Gwen wrapped an arm around Meg's waist, picked her up and got the fuck out of there. Once they passed the schoolyard, Gwen dropped Meg to the sidewalk and towed her home by the wrist, crushing sections of sidewalk one step at a time. Meg's feet stumbled at double time to keep up.

After school that day, Sara and Shepps entered the apartment, a bag of groceries dangling from the sock's mouth. The sock opened its maw and dropped the bag to the carpet. Sara opened her own mouth, stuck out her tongue and panted like a dog.

Sock Daddy brought chips and bananas and squishy white bread, she said.

Gwen and Meg were sifting through the remains of Sara's Halloween candy on the living room's patchy carpet. Sunflower seeds, raisins, black licorice. Not worth the effort to chew.

Bread, Meg exclaimed, both hands above her head.

Maybe Shepps'll make you peanut butter and jam, Gwen said.

Shepps complied. Sara, you hungry?

Sock Daddy wants sammich.

Sara lifted her off-white right hand and yapped her fingers open and closed. The sock had stretched as a result of its verbosity, each of Sara's fingers now fit into a grey oval at the sock's toes and the sock's heel sat up like a dorsal fin at Sara's wrist.

Sara, that's enough, Gwen said.

What? Sara said, sock hand dangled at her side, sock slouched at her wrist and suspended from her fingers like it didn't care if it hung on or fell to the floor.

Talking with the sock. It's annoying.

It's not me, Mommy. It's Sock Daddy.

Gwen got off the couch and lunged at Sara. She grabbed the end of the sock and dug in with her fingernails. Give me the sock, she said.

No, Mommy. Sara sheltered the sock under her shirt.

Shepps, help me, Gwen snarled.

Can I have the sock? Shepps said.

No. You don't like Sock Daddy.

Shepps shrugged and wiped a drip of sweat off his forehead with a plaid-covered wrist. Sock Daddy's alright, he said.

Sara pulled the sock out from under her shirt. She turned its fisted head to face Gwen. Youuu, the sock said, You don't like Sock Daddy. The sock mouthed a slice of bread and Sara stomped to her bedroom.

That night, Gwen retreated to the bath. She closed her eyes, her access to the outside world, and drifted underwater. She resurfaced to find Shepps unbuttoning his jeans above her. Pants off, Shepps grazed Gwen's fingers with his own.

Did I say you could come in?

Shepps' fingers froze. I'll give you privacy, he said.

I'm kidding. Gwen threw bubbles at Shepps. Don't take me so seriously.

Shepps tugged at his shirt and said nothing. Damian would've said, *You're such a bitch most of the time how do I know when you're kidding.* Damian would've ripped his jeans off and thrown them at Gwen so hard the zipper would bite her cheek. Then he would've grabbed her by the ear and not kissed her so much as sucked her out of herself through the mouth. But Shepps stood silently and waited for cues. How to be, how to please.

Gwen lifted her fingers and wrapped them around Shepps'. Don't ask, she said. Do what you want.

Shepps stepped into the bath and kneeled in front of Gwen, placed an arm around her. He lifted her to him and mouthed a nipple. He nosed her neck and she let her head fall back, hit the tub wall.

Sorry.

Don't be.

Shepps wedged a wet palm between Gwen's head and the wall. He leaned in and kissed her mouth, dank and unbrushed. She fisted a handful of his slick hair, pinched at the roots, and held his face close to hers.

I want you to hurt me, Gwen said.

Shepps stared, wide-eyed.

Smash my head against the wall.

I can't.

Pull my hair.

Shepps shook his head. He sat down, cross-legged in the tub, his hand still cradling Gwen's head. I can't do that, he said. I love you.

Gwen sat up and released her head from Shepps' protection. She drew her knees to her face, rested a cheek on them and looked at Shepps, hunched over himself amid the bubbles.

You don't love me, Gwen said. You don't want to make me happy.

From the hall, through the inch of opened bathroom door, an off-white triangle whispered, You want to be miserable.

Shepps pulled the door open, with more force than he'd offer a strand of Gwen's hair, to reveal Sara on the floor. Eyes closed, breath heavy, right arm lowering from the elbow like a spring-loaded lever.

When Sara first formed words, only Damian could get her to talk. Her first word was *Da*. She didn't bother uniting her lips to form an *m* until past age one. Damian called her Jellybean. He made her Froot Loop necklaces and licorice tiaras. He'd skip with her to the 7-Eleven for sugar sticks and cigarettes and then he'd float away at dusk to screech and twang and screw until he decided to cross their threshold again. For Sara, as for any other clueless girl, that was enough.

Sara only opened her mouth now to act as a medium for the sock. She sat tight-lipped and dour, lifting her right hand every now and then to let the sock pontificate. She'd jump Shepps' checker piece and say, Sock Daddy is suffocating here, or stop, mid-shoe Velcroing, to ask, Where's Sock Daddy's yellow pick?

Her lunch kit was littered with notes, all of which Gwen ignored. A Post-it cat stated: *We need to discuss the sock.* An inspirational duckling declared: *The sock is becoming a problem.* A ripped scrap of loose-leaf pleaded: *Would you consider removing it?*

Gwen kept Sara home on extended sick leave. First chicken pox, then measles, mumps, tuberculosis. To the school secretary, Shepps explained that Gwen was anti-vaccination. Oops, he said.

Sara would not let anyone near the right side of her body. The sock was a soggy goo that had not touched towel for weeks. What it had touched: bathwater, soap, shampoo, feces, urine, boogers, chocolate bars, Cheetos. It was a cornucopia of colours and textures. It attracted all manner of dust, crumbs and bug carcasses. Sara left a dribble of filth everywhere she and her right arm went.

I worry about her health, Shepps said. He pushed a hair chunk out of his eyes but it slid back across his greasy forehead to its original position.

Gwen was nested in bed with a bottle of vodka: Shepps, behind her, attempted a soup spoon but came out wooden. Meg lay with her shoulders at their feet, her head dangled off the edge of the bed. Her little legs flopped onto Gwen and Shepps' bums and her clumsy fingers plucked at their toes.

It's not so bad, Gwen said. I'm used to it now.

What about school?

We've only scraped the surface of childhood disease.

She doesn't even talk. Shepps raked his pasty fingers from Gwen's knee to hip, exfoliating her thigh with his crusty plaid cuff.

Ow. Do you ever wash that thing?

Shepps held cuff to face. Red plaid embellished with peanut butter, apricot jam, mayonnaise, egg yolk.

I haven't been to the laundromat in a while, he said.

There's a laundry room here, you know.

You've never shown me.

Figure it out. I'm out of clean underwear.

Sure. Shepps slugged himself away from Gwen. He stood up, then slumped toward a pile of soiled undergarments.

I didn't mean right now.

I have to go.

What do you mean?

To the Esso. I have a job.

Gwen levitated her head an inch from the bed.

You need to be here, she reminded him.

We need to pay rent.

This isn't even your place.

I want to help you, Gwen. But—

I don't need your help.

I'll leave if you want.

I never asked you to stay.

That night Gwen bathed Meg and Sara together. Meg attached a few of Gwen's stray hairs to the shampoo bottle and played mermaids with it. The sock was the enchanted white eel the mermaid rode on. Sara poked two fingers out of holes in the sock's toe bed, like cartoonish, bugged-out eyes. Gwen sloshed her hands through the water to create the tsunami required to advance their storyline.

Run for cover, Sara squealed. To the high cliffs of Mount Soaperest!

Gwen watched her two girls in the tub. How much space there was without Shepps. How uncluttered. How long would he be gone? How long would the inch of milk in the carton last? Could she get her old job back at the diner? The one she had seven years ago when she met Shepps and Damian, with the red lips and the purposefully scruffy hair and the tight-waisted skirts. She looked down her front. Lumpy. Could she go out in public at all?

Gwen tucked Sara in with genuine affection. And, with genuine affection, said, We need to get rid of the sock.

The sock hid under Sara's covers. Sara flapped one ear and then the other to her pillow. A firm no. Gwen sat beside Sara on her bed. She imagined Sara's little fingers pulling every thread of that sock into itself until there was nothing left.

Gwen stood up and said, Daddy doesn't want to come back.

Once Sara fell asleep, Gwen stood in her doorway and watched her torso rise and fall. The sock covered Sara's arm, bent above her head like a hanger. Gwen stepped into the room, to the foot of Sara's bed. Sara's breath stopped for a second, then resumed, slow and steady. Gwen kneeled on all fours and crawled to the side of Sara's bed. Sara rolled toward her. The sock arm rose, beaked through the air toward Gwen, and landed level with her face.

Grimy piece of shit, Gwen said to the sock. Sara's fingers twiddled inside of it. Gwen lay her head next to its face. How could you do this to me? Gwen whisper-screamed, through a clenched jaw, Fuck. You. She rested her forehead on the sock and cried. Sara snored. Gwen shook. Then she bit at a loose section of sock. Sara's arm lay flaccid. Gwen held the sock in her mouth, pulled it off Sara's arm. It hung from Gwen's mouth. She breathed through it, drooled like a rabid dog. She looked at Sara's right arm, bare and vulnerable.

Gwen crawled out of Sara's room, panting. She dropped the sock to the floor and used it to wipe the saliva from her mouth.

She wanted to rip it to shreds, pin it to the wall, wash it, feed it, eat it. She wanted to put it right back on Sara's arm.

Gwen shuffled to the bathroom, closed the door and turned on the light. The room was too bright, all of its contents—the bathing pink elephant on the wall, the grey soap scraps, the jar of Q-tips—exposed. Gwen lit a candle and turned off the light. She stared at herself in the mirror. She rolled her head to accentuate the shadows that fell from the hard angles of her face. Stuck out her tongue. Pulled her hair back from her face.

Dirty old sock, she said.

She put Damian's sock on her right hand. She yanked up until she felt her fingertips rebel at its periphery, an uneasy coating. She gathered the toe bed in her fist and raised it to the mirror.

You want to be miserable, the sock said. You asked for this.

Gwen sat on the counter and leaned against the wall. She pressed her socked palm to her nose. She bit at her socked wrist. She bit harder until she cried out, stuffed her mouth with fisted sock and smacked her head against the wall. The sock withdrew from her mouth, but stuck to her dry gums as her arm lowered, shed like a snake's skin. The sock hung from her lips and dangled over the candle's flame. Gwen tilted her head, back and forth over the flame until the end of the sock caught fire. It burned and curled and crept toward her lips. The smell of burnt polyester filled the bathroom. This is it. Gwen pulled the sock from her lips and dropped it to the sink. The end. But she couldn't. She turned on the cold water and swirled the sock in its pool of filth. She wrung it out and placed that burn-holed, ragged, crust-edged, damp thing back on her arm. The sock slid up her shirt, wet and slow like a slug. It tugged at her nipples and slithered between her breasts up against her throat. Gwen exhaled through her teeth and bottom lip. The sock smelled of rain-washed sidewalk vomit and burnt rubber. It yanked her head from side to side then choked her left wrist and pulled it toward the fork in her thighs. Gwen dropped her right leg to the floor, pressed the crown of her head to the wall, wrapped the toes of her left foot around counter's edge. She spread for the sock. She arched her back and rocked her hips until the faucet bit into her left hip. And the sock—wet and persistent.

You miss the way I made you feel.

Gwen awoke in bed, alone save for the sock now stuck to her forearm. No starfished Meg, no sliver of Shepps, apologetically teetered at the far edge of the mattress. Gwen sprang her torso erect, elbowed the windowsill. Shepps' van still sagged at the curb. She breathed out the ball of panic from her stomach. She breathed in, breathed out, stared at the stagnant van. A viscous goo glurped up her throat. That shadowed patch of asphalt was a slow and certain asphyxiation.

Mommy, open jam, Meg yelled from the kitchen. This, followed by a plop and a clink.

Me open all by yourself, said Meg.

Fuck, Gwen said into her pillow.

Meg's chubby legs encircled a pile of apricot jam on the kitchen floor. She dipped in chunks of squishy white bread, wiped them onto her cheeks and into her mouth.

Great, Meg. Now we have no jam.

No jam.

Gwen fingered and licked an apricot chunk.

No Sissy, said Meg.

What?

No Sissy.

What do you mean?

Meg pointed toward the hall. Sissy gone, she repeated.

Sara was not in her room. Her covers trailed off her bed from one dragging point. Gwen looked toward the apartment door. It was open a crack. Closet door, open. Sara's raincoat, gone. Gumboots, gone.

Gwen grabbed Meg's raincoat and a sweater long enough to cover her own granny-pantied bottom. Come on, Meg, she said.

I eat jam.

We need to find Sara.

Meg rose, plodded every appendage into the jam pile, and waddled over. Gwen scanned the stairwell for Sara, between the balusters, the window wells, under dislodged swaths of carpet. She looked for a nest of light-brown hair, a protrusion of pink rubber.

Outside the building, Gwen and Meg approached Shepps' van. The roof was down. He hadn't set up the loft bed. He hadn't slept there. Gwen lobbed a rotten banana peel from the pocket of her sweater at the van's side window. Meg laughed and threw bits of gravel and grass, pompoms and plastic beads from her pockets toward the van.

Gwen heaved Meg onto her back and paced the building's property. Surely Sara wouldn't stray farther. They combed blades of grass, planted themselves next to tree trunks, and scoured mobiles of branches with their fingers and eyes. Meg's hair was a tangle of cherry blossoms and fir needles. Gwen was a sweatered hunchback with a rattily cloaked crotch. She fell to her knees and plopped Meg to the ground.

I can't breathe, said Gwen. My ribs.

Meg poked at Gwen's ribs.

Where the hell is your sister?

Gwen curled into a boulder on the grass. Meg climbed atop the boulder, swirled her apricot-jammed palm into Gwen's hair. Gwen breathed what air existed between her knees and the earth. Surely Sara wouldn't stray farther.

Sissy, Meg said. Sissy.

Meg slid off Gwen, bum first. Gwen lifted her head.

Up the sidewalk toward them strode Shepps with a greasy paper bag in one hand and Sara's hand in the other.

Gwen rose and ran toward the two while Meg tripped and toddled behind. Gwen fell to her knees at Sara's feet. She cried and reached for Sara's thin calves. Sara pushed at Gwen's shoulders with all of her wiry might, pushed her to the ground.

You took Sock Daddy away, Sara yelled.

She stomped her feet. She grabbed at the end of the sock dangling from Gwen's right hand, but Gwen held firm. Gwen pried Sara's hands from the sock and held them in her own. Sara drummed at Gwen's chest with her fists and collapsed into her lap. She cried until Shepps pulled a doughnut out of the paper bag and gave it to her. He retrieved another and fed it to Meg's pudgy, pulsating fingers. He sat down beside Gwen and told her he'd found Sara by the van last night. That she was looking for the sock.

Where were you? Gwen said.

What?

When you found her. Were you out with someone?

Really, Gwen?

Forget it. Why didn't you get me a doughnut?

Shepps sat quietly for a long time. As long as it took for Sara and Meg to lick all the icing off their doughnuts and eat the rest in bird-sized allotments. Then he put a hand on Gwen's thigh and squeezed it in that paternal way of touching a once-familiar, now-taboo surface.

You need to drive away, Gwen said.

Will you be okay?

I don't know.

Shepps gave her that look again, smug pity. Smug pity mixed with relief and a touch of sadness. He released her thigh. He looked at her but said nothing. Too earnest for I love you, too sentimental for goodbye.

Gwen stood and watched the girls roll in the grass and tongue icing from the paper bag. She walked toward Shepps' van, the space that would soon replace it. She listened to the *put-put-put*, the van's passive-aggressive roar when Shepps turned the key. As he crawled away from her, Gwen threw the sock at his back window, which it lazily grazed before flopping into a catch basin at the side of the road. When the weather turned, it would disappear into the storm drain, the ocean. A different world.

Popular Girls

Sally called the day Madame Robertson gave a slide show on the Impressionists in French class. At Monet's *Water Lilies*, Sally raised her hand.

Weren't we supposed to have a quiz on imparfait today?

Alisha Fletcher coned her hands against her lips and chanted, Saaaaaa-llyyyyyy.

Then Trevor Blackburn sang, Sally Sally bo-bally she likes to keep the tally.

Trevor Blackburn was on the cusp of popularity. He wore mismatched socks and his forehead was dusted with just enough acne to make him approachable. He treated me like a kid sister, which meant he either wanted to kiss me or copy my homework. It was crucial I laugh at all his jokes in order to push him toward the former. But when I laughed, everyone laughed and I kicked it up a notch so it would seem perfectly acceptable to toss my head back and brush my hair across his fingertips on the desk behind mine. Sally looked as though she'd witnessed Madame Robertson pick All-Bran out of her teeth. An *Oh, the humanity!* sort of look.

When I answered the phone, without even saying hello back, Sally said, Why did you laugh at me?

Why did you bring up the quiz?

I studied all night.

So? Nobody else did.

I didn't think of that.

It was selfish, is all.

I didn't see what the Impressionists had to do with French class.

They were French.

They weren't verbs.

You don't interrupt a slide show. So not cool.

Are we still friends, Meg?

Why wouldn't we be?

You never talk to me at school.

You're always playing with soccer balls at lunch.

I guess. Alisha Fletcher must be nice.

She's fun.

Sally paused long enough for me to wonder if she was crying or choking or distracted by *Wheel of Fortune*.

You want to sleep over Saturday?

'Course, Sally. Yeah. Sure.

I hung up the phone to find Mom at the kitchen table, sucking peanut butter on Wonder Bread from her molars.

Was that Sally?

Uh-huh. I'm sleeping over at her place Saturday.

Good.

I was twelve years old, the age at which Mom needed only to say one word to enrage me. By *good*, she meant as long as I slept on an air mattress in Sally's bedroom I would remain in the safe, unalterable past. To Mom, Sally meant sweatpants and dolls and lemonade stands. If I hung out with my new friends from middle school I might wear eyeliner and ultra-low-rise jeans and go to night dances in the gymnasium. I might become popular like my sister Sara. Popular girls got into trouble. They skipped class and dated boys and had sex and abortions. They talked back to Mom and stopped getting the groceries for her. And when they did get the groceries they spent the milk money on *Rolling Stone* and the Hamburger Helper money on blue hair dye. When it was time to take Mom to her bank appointment, they said, *I'm watching* Buffy. Popular girls stared at the TV screen and said, *Meg can take you to your appointment. Meg does nothing but play dolls. Let Meg take you for a change.* And while Mom groped at the doorknob and said, *Meg's never done it, Meg doesn't know what to say to the bus driver, Meg's not old enough for this*, popular girls stood up as though they were going to relent or hug her, but they grabbed her by the shoulders and said, *I. Can't. Hear. My. Show.*

Mom licked peanut butter from her fingertips. You two used to be inseparable, she said.

I guess.

Used to dance to the Spice Girls in your underwear on the balcony, remember?

Yup.

Guess you won't be doing that on Saturday.

Mom stared at her fingertips, pressed them into one another and apart as though nostalgic for the peanut butter that once united them. Nothing was ever so good for Mom as the moment before. She was a constant reminder of the passage of time. Sally and I had grown up, we were different. Life would never again be as simple as it was when we hollered "Wannabe" in our panties to passersby. Those passersby had become real people who saw, judged and possibly praised what I did. My inventory of acceptable actions was diminishing. I would not have another moment of unselfconscious fun. This information should have been percolated to me through people I could later discount: Sex Ed. teachers, team captains, boys on skateboards.

That Saturday, Sally stood in the threshold of her home, a vulgar relapse into childhood. Spice Girls T-shirt worn in earnest, not irony, blonde hair as straight and untouched as when she was six. She hugged me and I smelled her skin, sweet and warm like jam on toast. A chunk of my mascara smudged onto her cheek and she wiped it with her fingertip.

You do have fuller lashes, she mumbled.

It's cry-proof too.

Handy.

Sally's house was a relic from our shared childhood. Same spill-resistant, vacuum-tracked carpet. Same wall of gold-marbled mirrors in the living room. Same momish mom. Same jar of cookies. Real, melt-in-your-mouth homemade cookies.

You girls want a snack?

Sally's mom leaned out of the kitchen, all ten fingertips wedged into her jeans pockets. She tried to push them in farther, but gave up when she hit the soft wall of flesh I'd once heard Sara refer to as a *gunt*. There were no visible bones on Sally's mom, the way a mom should be. She was the cushion between us and the awful world I knew I would eventually become, but in a grotesque alternate universe in which I was old and undesirable. Sally told her mom we weren't hungry, but I would've killed for one of her cookies. Sally grabbed for my hand and led me down the hall to her room.

What should we do? Sally said.

Alisha Fletcher never asked what we should do. She said we're going to the mall. We're trying on jewellery at Claire's. We're slipping earrings into your backpack and leaving the store. We're acting cool or we'll get caught.

Dunno, I said.

I wanted to dissect Trevor Blackburn. How he used the perfect amount of hair gel, like Ricky Martin. How he was so cool he made braces cool. How he had touched me on the shoulder in French class to ask for a pencil. I knew he had pencils of his own. Trevor Blackburn was nothing but prepared. But if Sally and I had ever discussed boys, it was to whine about their tendencies toward hair-pulling and potty talk. I didn't know whether Sally's opinion had changed and I was too afraid to ask. I wanted to emerge from the purgatory between childhood and adolescence headfirst, and it seemed one false move with Sally would hurl me, breech, into my future.

How about Barbies? I suggested.

Sally seemed relieved. She led me downstairs to the play-room—which she still labelled, shamelessly, The Playroom—and set up one of our usual scenarios. Barbie and her friends were at school. Sally pulled out some of her brother's G.I. Joes.

Schools have boys, right, Sally said.

Unfortunately.

Maybe there's a school dance.

And they have to go with a boy.

Skipper's gonna freak, Sally squealed.

Sally was pretty tame with Skipper. She put Skipper's hands on G.I. Joe's shoulders while they danced to her Destiny's Child CD. My Barbie shoved her plastic digits down her partner's pants. I peeked through my frizz of brown curls for Sally's reaction. She was oblivious, her eyes trained on the miniature couple under her control, her head tilted and lips parted to sing along to a love song she didn't understand.

Wanna do something else? Sally said. She laid her dolls on the carpet and rose to her hands and knees, squishing the plastic couple beneath her palms. Perhaps we were there for the same reasons. An homage to a history we were too afraid, too naïve, to let go of.

Sally crawled across the room and opened a baby-blue trunk. We used to call it the Tickle Trunk in the days when Mr. Dressup held heroic status. When the ability to make anything out of construction paper and to maintain an even temper for half an hour were all it took to turn our cranks. Sally pulled out handfuls of silver platform shoes and floral-printed string bikinis.

Your mom used to fit these?

Yeah, before she was a mom.

Sally criss-crossed her arms and pulled her T-shirt over her head. She leaned, topless, over the web of spandex before her and scooped out a faded brown bikini top. It had firm cups and looked like a giant moth dancing from Sally's finger. I tried not to look at Sally's chest. It had mutated since we'd last seen each other naked. It protruded from her ribs, swayed, lifted and landed when she moved. It had bra-filling potential. She tied the bikini strings behind her neck and shoulder blades and tucked a fist into each cup.

Look, I'm my mom, she said.

You already have boobs, I said.

So do you, a bit.

Judging from my mom, this is as big as they'll get.

Judging from my mom, I'll be a whole lot bigger. Everywhere.

I dipped an arm into the trunk and rifled through the musty disco-dance party. I pulled out a mint-green nightie fashioned from layers of netting and held together by sequined shoulder straps. A marshmallow of a dress, something a faerie vixen would wear, Tinkerbell or Courtney Love, like on that poster in Sara's room with her scabby knocked knees, raccoon eyes and swollen bottom lip.

I think my mom wore that on her honeymoon, Sally said.

It's pretty hot.

I put it on over my head and squatted to shimmy off my shorts and T-shirt under a cloak of tulle. Perhaps I was embarrassed that the only change I had undergone since we last saw each other naked was mental. I wished Sally's chest was like mine—a couple of mosquito bites on a ladder of ribs. But Sally's chest was unavoidable.

I threw a hot-pink tube top at Sally and told her to wear it as a skirt. You'll look so Posh Spice, I said.

The top hit Sally's face and fell to the floor. She lifted a hand slowly to her nose then sunk, straight-legged, to pull the top up along her floppy calves, then thighs, which she lifted and dropped in tandem. She looked like a mermaid.

Okay. I'm Courtney and you're my neighbour, Madison. Madison's this boring mom and Courtney is this divorcee who wants to get it on with Brad, the mailman.

Get it on?

Like, go on a date.

What do they get on?

It. You know: *it*. I lounged on the couch, Manet's *Olympia* with legs crossed at the calves. Madison, be a dear and fetch me a vodka screwdriver?

Is that a sour candy?

Never mind. Here comes Brad. Isn't he a dreamboat?

Oh, Courtney! If my husband could hear us talk.

That bore? You should have an affair with Brad. But not until I'm done with him.

I would never. I love my husband.

Sally, you're killing the game.

Sorry. I don't know what you want me to say.

Say what you want.

Truth was, I didn't want Sally to say what she wanted, or what I wanted. I wanted her to show me what I wanted.

Maybe we should go to the 7-Eleven and get soft serve.

Like this?

Yeah, it'll be fun.

Sally looked down at her bikini top, sagging under her collarbones. The miniskirt swaddled her hips below her arched back and tummy.

I can kind of see your underwear, she said.

I tugged at the bottom of my nightie. It's Little Miss underwear, I said. Little Miss Naughty. It's funny.

I picked up two pairs of sequined, five-inch platform shoes and tossed one to Sally. We headed outside, a wobbly parade. An old lady with a wiener dog *tsk-tsk*ed at us and I knew this meant we were teenagers. If we were girls she would've cocked her head and told us how darling we were.

Behind the counter of the 7-Eleven, two boys gazed at skater mags and slurped bright-orange Big Gulps. My stomach dropped. They went to Vic High. My sister's friend's brother played soccer with them. They were popular. They looked up at us and snickered and I steered Sally to the soft-serve machine.

Courtney dear, I hope this won't ruin our figures, Sally said, far too loudly.

I glanced over at the boys to see if they heard, but at the same time moved my hand so the ice cream flowed onto my forearms. Sally burst out laughing and swatted me with napkins.

Hey, c'mere, one of the boys said. He held up a wad of paper towel.

I walked over and stretched my arms out to him.

You girls playing dress-up or what? The boy knelt to my level and scrubbed at my arm in a circular motion as though buffing a windshield.

I didn't answer. A boy was touching my arms. This was nothing like a blotting from Mom's spit-moistened tissues.

Your name's Courtney?

I nodded.

I'm Mark.

I smiled.

Do you talk?

I nodded.

Mark had greasy blond hair tucked behind his ears and wore a faded Green Day T-shirt and jeans baggy enough to display a good four inches of boxer above the waist.

When Mark had wiped the ice cream from my forearms, he rose from his squat then paused distinctively. I looked down and saw that, in my hunched position, my chest was completely uncovered by my nightie's neckline. His eyes were on my nipples. *My* prepubescent, chocolate-chip nipples.

When his eyes moved away, I tried to meet them so I could raise my eyebrows and pout like Courtney Love but he didn't look me in the eye.

He smacked my shoulder and said, Nice panties.

When we left the store, Sally crossed her arms as best she could with an ice cream cone in one hand and said, Meg, he was looking at your chest.

I know.

Looking.

So?

Don't you feel used?

There's nothing to see.

What I couldn't say to Sally was that I felt noticed. I felt real. I also felt used, but the other two feelings trumped that one. We walked home in silence, our mouths immersed in ice cream. Sally probably wasn't imagining if this was what it was like to kiss a boy. She probably wasn't wondering if this was what a penis felt like against her tongue, only colder. If boys hadn't invaded my mind, I would've thought about how the flavour vanilla had strayed so far from the bean itself that anything with sugar and no other flavouring was called "vanilla." Or maybe I would've calculated in my head how long ice cream would take to melt in various temperatures and on various surfaces. Sun-soaked pavement in June versus the middle of the desert in December versus on a train heading north at sixty kilometres per hour about to collide with a camel.

Sally crunched on her cone and said, What are you thinking about?

Algebra.

Your bra?

What? No.

You don't wear one?

My sister gave me her old one. I kinda hate it.

My mom says I need one for sports.

I have like no boobs.

The guy at 7-Eleven didn't think so.

Saaa-lly.

We giggled. I nudged Sally and a gooey chunk of my ice cream blobbed onto her calf. She toppled over her platform heel and onto someone's yard.

We wiped her calf in the grass and I said, Maybe we should go back and get Mark to lick it off for you.

I felt high like I did with Alisha Fletcher. Someone who depleted the oxygen to my brain.

I would never let that perv touch me, Sally said.

She didn't say it out of jealousy. Jealousy was coveted. This was naïveté engendered from a mother who darns socks and picks you up from the mall when you miss the bus and attends your dance recitals. Sally's mom would hold her hand through puberty, answer questions, share embarrassing first-date stories, show her how to operate a razor and a tampon. The times I had plucked up the courage to ask Mom a question about what *actually* happens when you have sex or what does it mean when a boy messes up your hair in a rough way and then says, *You look pretty like that*, she would flop her head back, exhale through an open mouth, and say, *Meg, I'm not the one to ask*. Alisha Fletcher's mom worked night shifts and gave her cold pizza and Coke in her lunch. With Alisha, I could hold my peanut butter and jam on stale Wonder Bread sandwiches and my trail of unsigned permission forms and report cards as a point of pride. Popular girls had to be motherless.

My sister showed up at Sally's door after breakfast the next morning. She wore tight black jeans and an old seventies ringer tee that said *Wolftrap Lives*. Mom called these her street-person clothes but I only wished I had the flippancy to dress like her.

Let's go, Meggers.

I can walk home on my own.

Mom was all freaking out. She wanted me to come get you.

Sally's mom walked into the entryway, wooden spoon in hand, and asked Sara if she wanted any eggs.

No thanks, Mrs. G.

You sure? It's no trouble at all, sweetie.

Sally's mom smiled, plump and rosy cheeked, and for the first time I felt anger rather than envy. It seemed she wanted to rub in the fact that our mom didn't cook eggs, or anything that didn't reside, dehydrated, in a box.

Nnnnnoooo thanks, Mrs. G. My sister leaned back with her foot up against the door jamb.

I shimmied my feet into my shoes and smacked Sally's shoulder the way Mark had smacked mine. Thanks, Sally. I'll see ya.

Yeah, she said. See you around.

I didn't want *See you around*. I wanted *When can I see you again?* Attempted hellos met with ambivalent pass-bys. Longing looks in French class. Contrived reasons to talk to me: a maxi-pad to borrow, homework comparisons, a note-passing middleman.

I gave her my most aloof, For sure, and left before she could respond.

On our way home from Sally's, my sister walked a consistent metre in front of me, no matter how I hurried to catch up.

Hey, Sara, I yelled.

What?

Is Mom—did she have a party last night?

She's fine, Meg. She was pissing me off with her questions, is all.

Sure?

Yeah. Don't worry, kid. Sara put her arm on my shoulder for almost two seconds, but then pretended to brush dirt off my T-shirt.

I like your shirt. What does Wolftrap mean?

It's just bullshit, Meg. It could say anything.

Can I borrow it?

You can rip it off my dead body.

Hey, Sara?

Yeah?

What does it mean when a boy looks at you?

Looks at *you*?

Or anyone. Like, down your shirt.

Sara laughed and spun to face me. Meg, you little slut.

She held her hand up like a stop sign in front of me and I thought she was going to hit me. I flinched and drew my hands to shelter my face. Sara waited for my hand to meet hers. Her mouth was open, lips curved, her eyes warm. The face she wore for birds who'd flown into our balcony window or for any mention of our absent father. The face she wore for the flawed and the reckless. The unacceptable.

The Postcard

I haven't seen my father, in body or spirit, since I was two years old, but here he is on an otherwise unremarkable February day in the form of a stamped, all-white rectangle embellished with the words *Winnipeg in Winter* in black. On the backside of the postcard, his message reads:

> *Jellybean & Co.,*
> *Passing through Winnipeg. Thinking of you.*
> *Dad*

Sara arrives home in a teen angst–induced haze. She stumbles over my sneakers and plants her hands on my shoulders.

Swear to God, Meg. I'm so done with this place.

Sara is almost eighteen and is technically too old to run away, but she threatens to leave me and Mom whenever we're out of soy milk or hot water or Fruit Roll-Ups. Or if she burns her toast or bites her tongue or her hair won't sit right. The farthest she's gone is to her friend Rita's for a couple of nights. Mom was working late shifts at the coffee shop and when Sara returned, all Mom said was: So that's why the bathroom's been so available.

What's that? Sara says.

I hold up the postcard, winter side out. It's from our father, I say.

Sara yanks the postcard from my hand, quick enough to scratch my finger webbing. Our father left twelve years ago when Sara was six—old enough to know him. He nicknamed her Jellybean. Mom still calls her JB, but not in a nicknamey way. *Hey JB, do you plan to vacuum the apartment or are we plotting a zen garden?*

Mom opens the door, trips over my sneakers, says, Fuck, Meg, and sits at the kitchen table followed by Gary, this guy who trails her home from the coffee shop every other day. Mom told us Gary's a transient, which means he has no fixed address. This is different from a homeless person. Homeless people eat hand-outs. Gary eats with friends. Homeless people dumpster dive for bottles. Gary is a professional recycler. Homeless people push shopping carts. Gary carries a backpack. Homeless people ride stolen bikes. Gary rides a found skateboard. Homeless people are trapped. Gary is free.

Sara disapproves of Gary in the same way she disapproves of authority figures and animal products. When Mom brings home day-olds from the coffee shop, Sara will ask if they were made with animal cruelty. If Gary's there, Mom is snarky. *Yes, Sara. On my way to the coffee shop, I strangled a bunny with my bare hands.* When Gary isn't around, Mom's quieter. She'll look at Sara, sigh, and flick the baking from counter to garbage.

The four of us hover at each corner of the postcard. Sara traces lazy fingerprints through Winnipeg's winterscape, Gary pinches and eats crumbs off the kitchen table, Mom repeats my father's blasphemous lines—*Passing through! Thinking of you!*—and I stare at the words, *& Co.*

Did he forget my name? I sit next to Sara and she lets me have a bite of her granola bar, which means she really pities me. Sara doesn't let just anyone's saliva mingle with her own.

You were only two.

So, forgettable?

Mom grabs the postcard and fans herself with it. Why can't he let us forget him?

Is he coming back? I say.

No, Mom says.

Then why would he send this? Sara says.

So we know we're on his mind, I say.

So he stays on our minds, Mom says. Egomaniac.

He could be headed west, Sara says.

Mom stands behind Gary and wraps her hands around his waist so he looks a bit like a four-armed insect. A cockroach. She says, Who'd want to leave Winnipeg in Winter for Victoria?

Sara rolls her eyes. Yeah, Mom. Why on earth would Dad rather be in Winnipeg?

Mom turns tomatoey and releases Gary. Why is the sky blue, Sara? Why is your hair brown?

Those questions have scientific answers, Sara says.

Mom exhales long and slow through pursed lips. She looks at Sara, panicked, like she's trying hard not to go apeshit in front of Gary.

Look it up in the dictionary then, she says. Under dickhead. Then she says, Sorry, Meg.

Mom stomps into the living room and turns on *Jeopardy!* Gary follows her. He shouts out answers, always wrong. Every time, Mom reminds him to say *What is* first.

—

From Valentine's to St. Patrick's Day, the postcard has lived in Sara's room, wedged into a chilly white corner of her mirror. After school, before she gets home, I take it out to analyze my father's handwriting. It could belong to one of the boys in my class. The ones who cheat off Sally Greene's pop quizzes and write book reports on *Calvin and Hobbes*.

Gary's the one who catches me in Sara's room, on her bed with the postcard.

She probably wouldn't dig this, he says, and throws his chin toward me.

The truck of his skateboard dangles from the pit of his first two fingers. He pulls his greasy blond hair up against his forehead with yellowed fingers and scratches his eleven-o'clock shadow. He wears his filth the way the girls at school wear eyeliner. Brushed and clean-shaven, he'd be boring and unemployed, but grungy guys get free day-olds from the coffee shop and sleepovers with the servers. I want him to sit on the bed with me, close enough to feel the sticky heat from the sleeve of his flannel shirt. I want him to cradle the postcard, to study its script, explain it to me. *See the long line on his* y? *It's pointing west.* Then Gary might rest his palm on top of my hand. He might look me in the eyes and squeeze it like I've seen him squeeze Mom's hand, their fingers zippered, their pendulum arms.

I'm allowed to look.

He jiggles his skateboard. Don't want to anger the beast.

It's mine too.

I know, kid. Forget it. Not my business.

I tuck the postcard into the waistband of my jeans and stride toward the door.

My sister's not a beast, I say, and Gary backs out to let me pass.

Sara knows the postcard is missing. A cacophony of thrown books and billowed sheets, a stampede of palms on hardwood percolates through my wall. I sit inside my room atop my math book where I've hidden the postcard, still and silent as though Sara's an orc who'll attack once aware of my presence. I don't know whether this incubation is my attempt to be close to my father or to punish Sara for the closeness she's had.

I risk taking the postcard to school because it won't be real until Alisha Fletcher sees it.

My dad visits every Sunday, she says.

You have a father?

Hardly.

What do you guys do?

Nothing. He takes me to the Beacon Drive-In and buys me ice cream like I'm six. And he talks about the stock market. On his cellphone. To other people.

Sorry.

Don't be.

Alisha squeezes my thigh. I turn to see Matt Ainsley at three o' clock. He's the kind of guy you can feel approaching before he's visible. He's that cool. Matt Ainsley resides twenty-four lockers down the hall from me. Between Math and Language Arts, I stare at him through a rust hole in my locker door, like a non-psychotic Norman Bates. He stacks his books in order of descending surface area then pins them between his hip bone and three or four fingers—nonchalant, not the way I clasp my books to my chest with two crossed arms, hermetically sealing myself from the high school atmosphere with paper, coil and cardboard.

Is that a detention slip? Matt Ainsley points at the postcard.

It's from Meg's father. Alisha turns to face him and tugs at the hem of her shirt so it slips off one shoulder. Her bra strap is turquoise, which is beyond sexy.

Winnipeg in Winter, Matt Ainsley says. He flips over the postcard and reads my father's message. Your father's gone?

Yeah, I say.

Matt Ainsley lays the postcard on my lap. The tip of one of his fingers touches my wrist. My parents are so boring, he says.

Meg's mom is dating a homeless guy.

He's actually transient.

Cool, Matt Ainsley says. Then Matt Ainsley palms my shoulder. You're doing good in Socials, right? You did that presentation on the sufferers?

Suffragettes?

I gotta present the September Crisis on Monday.

October?

No, Monday.

Uh-huh.

Think you could help me out? Saturday night?

Matt Ainsley flicks an errant hair out of his eye with a whole-head, Tourette's-style motion. I nod, speechless. Alisha Fletcher slides a half inch away from me. A small but pronounced distance.

Saturday night, I show up at Matt Ainsley's with a carnation pinned to my shirt over my budding chest. He lives in Fairfield, by the ocean, in a large heritage home that could've been owned by a Scotsman named James now immortalized in street signs—Douglas,

Yates, Dunsmuir. The path to the front door is suspiciously hedge heavy, like a moustached politician. Matt Ainsley's mom answers the door and guides me to the rec room with a bowl of baked beans. Matt Ainsley awaits me with a bean-steamed crotch and a *Notting Hill* DVD. Alisha Fletcher swears Julia Roberts movies are a sure sign a guy wants to get with you. She once made out with Darren Carter for the duration of *Pretty Woman*.

The movie is on low and all I hear is the clink of our spoons. The plight of the Québécois will not feature on tonight's menu. I flick at my carnation. Would it be worse to remove it, thus admitting to wardrobe anxiety or to leave it on, thus admitting to a nerdy fascination with Pierre Elliott Trudeau? I have no appetite for baked beans. I have no appetite for Matt Ainsley's appetite for baked beans. I don't want to witness him slurp, smack, swallow—be so disgustingly human.

Not hungry? He wipes his mouth downward like he's doing that happy-face/sad-face clown act.

Uh-uh.

Hugh Grant's kind of a d-bag, eh?

My sister thinks he's hot.

Do you?

I dunno. He's like thirty.

Matt Ainsley puts his hand on my shoulder. The same motion performed at school a couple days ago but this time there's nothing to stop an elaboration—authority figures, self-conscious peers, public nudity laws.

It feels like an hour since either of us has spoken. I wait for Julia Roberts to say something I can comment on but this movie is all about fear of intimacy. I fear the ascent of Matt Ainsley's hand under my carnation, about to hit nipple. Nippular contact must be the transition from first to second base. I have never asked Alisha Fletcher for specifics. I need to swallow a lot. My swallowing is louder than it has ever been. I store the saliva in my mouth and count to twenty before I swallow again.

Matt Ainsely's sofa is black leather. There's doctor's-office art up on the walls. Framed watercolours of gardens and non-threatening forest creatures: deer, squirrels, the mighty beaver. Mom decorates our apartment with thumbtacked newspaper clippings, fortune cookie fortunes and found items like grocery lists, love letters and ATM statements. She says it makes her feel a part of a greater whole to be surrounded by other people's lives. To which Sara will respond, *Why don't you surround yourself with other people?* And Mom will deflate.

Matt Ainsley scooches a few inches closer to me. His grey sweatshorts shimmy up his thigh, which squeaks conspicuously against the leather. The downy flesh revealed brings to mind a piglet's belly, or a portly, Speedoed neighbour. Matt Ainsley's lips are big and dry and he covers my whole mouth with them. His tongue and my tongue can't figure out this dance. He has one arm hooked around my neck like a vice while his fingers twiddle under my bra, bobbing my Trudeau flower against my breast pocket. His other hand sneaks down the front of my pants. Where does he learn these things? His finger is cold. It feels like he's searching for his keys inside of me.

Alisha Fletcher will want details on Monday. I have to strad-dle the line between frigid and slut. I'll tell her how he fumbled for my nipple while choking me in his elbow pit for like ten min-utes and never quite reached. That will make her laugh. I won't tell her I avoided his zipper. Or that, when he tried to pull my pants down farther, I pressed his hand against my thigh to stop him. He said, What's up, baby, and all I could think was, *Don't call me baby. You didn't know my name a week ago.* And *Why is* this *the first activity that comes to a boy's mind when he has a girl in his basement?* I'd rather play checkers. I get up and tell Matt Ainsley that I have to go and I step in my bowl of baked beans. And Matt Ainsley lies back on the couch. Silent. I say, Thanks for the beans, and Matt Ainsley lies on the couch and says, Later, but to Julia Roberts.

Sunday is grocery day. Mom calls it Family Fun Day, though only she and I participate and it doesn't fit the standard definition of fun. Sunday is the day Sara locks herself in her room, burns incense, and plays Le Tigre at top volume. Mom won't admit to it, but she's afraid of the unexpected world outside our apartment. She gets dressed before bed on Saturday night so she doesn't have time to change her mind about leaving the house Sunday morning. Bright-red jeans and a denim button-up shirt. The height of fashion twelve years ago when the Grocery Shopping Outfit came to be. Once, I told her the outfit brings attention to us but that made her sigh, cross her arms, tap her fingers on the kitchen counter, then rub her palms together. She answered in her quiet, psycho-mom voice.

What do you suggest I wear, Meg?

I said, Forget it, but she listed off a series of outfits, each one less plausible.

A white sheet? A unitard made of soup can labels for camouflage? My wedding dress?

We didn't get groceries that week. We lived off day-olds from the coffee shop and a carton of milk I bought at the 7-Eleven with our laundry quarters. I was borderline scorbutic. Sara, as far as I could tell, didn't eat that week. She told me cows were the unwilling nursemaids to our carnivorous society.

When Mom wakes up, she muffles me with a granola bar and tells me to get dressed, get dressed, get dressed. While Mom fumbles with her shoes, I run to my room and flip through my math book to make sure the postcard is still there. Has Sara not bothered to look here because I'm insignificant? Or maybe she has. Maybe she knows exactly where it is and it is she who's torturing me. I push my math book under my bed and cover it with dirty underwear.

Mom and I walk down Fort to Cook. Turn right and walk two blocks to Yates. Left on Yates until we hit the market. If the accordion man is out front, we give him a loonie. If it's the loud, atonal girl with messy yellow hair, Mom says, *She's got guts*, but we don't encourage her financially. Every week, as we're about to enter the market, Mom tells me to go ahead because she has an errand. She joins me twenty minutes later, her backpack lumpy with vodka bottles, and I pretend I don't notice. I weave through the aisles from Frozen Foods to the Meat Counter. Mom usually joins me in Baking Needs, where I stock up on marshmallows and decorative sprinkles. Mom says sprinkles make even Kraft Dinner festive.

I see a flash of plaid in the junk food aisle. Gary drags his feet with his arm draped around a girl. Her hair's in braids and she laughs with her head back like Gary's not funny but she wants him to be. The lines around her eyes disappear when her lips flatline. Not like Mom's.

He holds his hand up like a sunshade. Hey Meg, what's happening?

Groceries. I walk toward him and Woodstock Barbie.

Where's your mom? Gary hugs me, and crunches a bit of my hair in his hand. His chin touches my neck in a big brother sort of way. It gives me roller-coaster stomach.

I point my thumb toward the exit. Errands, I say.

Meeting her parole officer? Gary says.

I don't know what a parole officer is, but I can tell by the tilt of Woodstock Barbie's laughing head that he's making fun of Mom. I tell Gary I'll see him around and don't even look him in the eye.

When I get to one of the two acceptable checkout ladies—the short one with the tidy ponytail and purple eyeshadow or the chubby girl with the blonde bob, both quick and untalkative, non-judgmental—Mom still hasn't arrived. I leave the basket with Purple Eyeshadow and check outside.

I find Mom at the corner of Yates and Cook, ploughing home.

Mom, I yell.

She stops, hands to hips and I run up to meet her. She exhales. Either from exertion or she's on her way to psycho-mom. I saw you with Gary and some girl, she says.

I only said hello.

Was she pretty?

In a boring way.

Mom fists two chunks of her dangling hair and pulls at them like floppy dog ears. Her eyes are blank and her cheeks release toward the ground.

I wobble my head to try and catch Mom's dead eyes. Did you guys break up?

Mom shakes her head. We were never.

Should I go pay for our stuff?

Good girl. Mom blindly hands me her wallet and continues home.

Since I was two years old, I've walked this route beside Mom and her outfit, too close to see her. It droops off Mom's frame, her frayed jean cuffs rake the sidewalk behind her. I watch until she's small enough to be unrecognizable. She doesn't look back once.

Monday, pre–first period bell, Alisha Fletcher guides me into the girls' bathroom, third stall. The one that's all about Lisa L. and Shane F. in Tangerine Dream nail polish. *Lisa L. hearts Shane F. Shane F. is a megaloser. Lisa L. + Shane F. 4ever.*

Alisha jerks her hips left to right and raises her thong slightly above the waistline of her jeans. I have so much to learn from this girl. My panties still cover cheek.

You barfed on him.

Who?

Matt Ainsley.

What?

There's a rumour.

Serious?

Alisha has one hand up on the stall door, the opposite hip thrust out. His parents are out of town this weekend, she says. Be at the water fountain before fifth. He'll for sure walk by on his way to PE. You don't want to be The Girl Who Barfed.

Pre-fifth period. Water fountain. Many drinks. Many unnecessary shoe-tyings. The school secretary comes out and asks if I'm okay. That's the worst insult. Goody-goodies take acceptable pauses. Cool kids loiter. I feel Matt Ainsley approach, but like a slop of oatmeal in my stomach rather than warm milk down my spine. His jeans are factory degraded. Fake-real holes and wear marks. I'd prefer someone who wears out his own jeans.

But when he walks up he nods at me. The *whassup* nod. And I think he's hot again. He says hey and I say hey back.

You missed the end of the movie.

Was it unpredictable?

No.

I thought maybe Hugh Grant would sell his bookstore and become a UFC champ.

Matt Ainsley takes a drink from the fountain and says, My parents are out of town Friday.

Cool.

You should come over.

A drop of water rides Matt Ainsley's chin and he lets it. Like no drop of water is going to take him down.

Sure.

He slaps his hand on my hip like it's his to touch, like he's my boyfriend.

Gary hasn't come over for a week. Not even to eat Froot Loops and use the bathroom. Mom has this shruggy way about her when she enters the apartment now, like Gary was proof she was worthwhile. But today Mom arrives with Gary behind her, his hand on her back. Their mouths are closed, like a grim ventriloquist act. He's not in plaid and he keeps his sunglasses on, even in the apartment. Mom goes to her room and Gary sits at the kitchen table across from me. Silent, like we've been asked if we have anything to say for ourselves in the principal's office.

Gary, when you were in high school, if a girl came over and you kissed and stuff but then she left for no reason, would you tell people she barfed?

What? His sunglasses slide down his nose.

Never mind.

Stay away from boys.

You're a boy.

Gary removes his sunglasses and sucks on one of the tips. Boys like that one, he says.

Gary lifts one foot onto the kitchen table and tips his chair back like Matt Ainsley would, only there's no teacher to scold him about the safety of himself and his peers.

Mom comes out of her room with what looks like the contents of a free box in her arms: a few scratched CDs and a moth-devoured T-shirt. She drops it on the table but then gives Gary a can of soup and a cookie and tells him to take care of himself in a momish voice. Like other people's moms. Gary says, You sure about this, and Mom nods. I know this is the last time I'll see Gary. Even though I will see him because he's always hanging around Mom's coffee shop.

When the door closes Mom stares straight ahead without moving or even blinking. Silent-mom. Statue-mom. I say, It's okay and You'll be fine, but I don't think she hears me.

I walk down the hall to Sara's door, even though it's a Meg-free zone. Sara says, Go away, before I even knock.

I have the postcard, I say.

She opens the door. Let's see.

It's in my room.

Sara steps one foot out of her doorway and watches me scurry into my room to retrieve the postcard. Sleeping over the postcard hasn't brought me closer to him, hasn't filled any father-sized void. It has only fattened me with a secret. I hand it to Sara.

She snatches it like a ticket-taker. You little bitch.

I push the door open and sit on her floor. Gary's gone, I say, and I start to cry.

Sara sits beside me and lets me cry into her neck.

He was just some douche, Meg.

He made Mom happy. Sometimes.

He did look good in plaid.

His teeth were gross.

He models for those warning labels on smoke packs.

Sara lets me laugh into her neck then she says, Okay Meggers, that's enough fluid, and pushes me off.

He's on me. Matt Ainsley's on me and there's no movie this time. No Julia Roberts. No rec room, no baked beans, just Hey Meg and into his bedroom. At least we're under the sheets. They're soft and black. His mom cares about home decor and Lysol and square meals. Block parties. He undoes my shirt and rubs his hand along the lace of my bra like he's de-callousing his palm. He fish-bites my throat and dog-humps my leg. He undoes my belt buckle, my button, my zipper and I wriggle my legs to help my pants off. He stands and takes off his pants. It's happening this time. He fumbles with his pants over his heels. He looks up, above me with blank, determined eyes and jumps foot to foot like a sprinter at his marks. I wish he'd go faster. I don't want time to think, *Why am I here, why am I doing this*. Matt Ainsley has a condom and I'm glad he does because I wouldn't have said anything. He pinches the top like we learned in Sex Ed. He lowers down, eyes closed now, lips flat and tight over his teeth. He doesn't kiss me, he's just in me. Matt Ainsley is in me. He's a Vic High celebrity and he feels like a roll of saran wrap slamming inside me but he also feels like the right thing to do. The cool thing to do. He grunts and whimpers a bit and I think he's done. I think it's over. He's still, dead weight. Is it over? Yes.

He takes off the condom and ties it, pinches his deposit through the latex.

He puts on his pants and says, Maybe we'll do this again.

I know that means he's not my boyfriend, but he's with me now.

Sara's door is open a crack. When Sara's door opens, it's as if the refrigerator is unsealed. It deregulates the atmosphere in the apartment. She looks at me and I flinch, even though the hallway is neutral territory.

Come in. But be quiet. You want anything? She sweeps her right arm across her room like one of those Janices on *The Price Is Right*.

Don't you?

No room. She points to her backpack.

Where are you going?

Wherever.

Why?

Why stay?

I can't answer. Every sentence contains a *should* and Sara doesn't deal in *should*s.

I'll be alone with Mom.

Sara laughs. Sorry about that.

You're trying to find him? I point to our father's postcard poking from the top of Sara's backpack.

He's unfindable.

Sara sits, legs straddled around her backpack, and doesn't talk for ten breaths. She crosses her arms in a way so much like Mom it makes my stomach drop. I flick at a loose corner of the poster beside me. *No Matter Where You Go, There You Are.*

You are here, I say.

Not for long, she says.

Sara gets up and stumbles over the egg-shaped hole in her hardwood that used to swallow my marbles and Barbies' high heels. She plants her feet in the doorway as though waiting to be compelled to stay. I sift through closing statements in my mind. *Don't go. I'll miss you.*

Do I look like a woman now?

Sara looks at me with wide, wet eyes. You look like you're trying to be a woman, Meggie.

So do you.

Sara laughs. She takes off her backpack, opens it and pulls out a T-shirt. She throws it at me and says, Don't let Mom give you a hard time. Then she grabs her backpack and walks away.

I uncrumple the shirt and sink to the floor. It's her *Wolftrap Lives* ringer tee. The one that, two years ago, she told me I could rip off her dead body.

Room and Board

The mulleted man with his nose wedged into the back of my seat chants an Oilers cheer while the Martian child across the aisle barfs into bags his mother has collected from this bus's seat backs—all but one. When she snaked her arm into the mesh pocket at my knees I told her that her kid's not the only ralpher on this bus. Then I inflated my cheeks and folded over my seat arm toward her.

Their pile of twist-tied puke packages has now dampened my desire to head farther east. So I leave this aluminum shoebox of Axe for Men and congealing tuna-fish-sandwich air at Edmonton, Alberta: City of Champions, home to the Oilers, the murky waters of the North Saskatchewan River, and the mulleted man, whom I follow across said river over a homely, suicide-high bridge.

My guide takes me to an animal trail rippled with roots and overprotective branches in the ravine on the other side. This could be the path to a hot bowl of soup. This could be the path to his lair, where he plans to maim me with scythes and snow shovels and other prairie tools. I choose sidewalk, streetlights, billboards instead. I choose Rebar, a club pulsing with punk. I slip in without paying cover, which is easy when you have a penetrating stare and a blurred dark birthmark on the inside of your left wrist.

It's an all-ages show so the room is full of prepubescent boys who smell of mother's milk and unfledged body odour. And little girls with barrette-speckled heads and baggy skate pants, their belts like leather lips puckered to swallow them whole. At eighteen, I'm bigger than everyone and queen of the mosh pit until some guy with tassels of dark hair and Docs the size of Montreal stomps on my face. He falls to his knees and plants a palm to the floor on either side of my head to protect me from further stampeding. He shakes his head and moves his lips, probably to tell me how clumsy and sorry he is, but his speech is quashed by the throbbing bass line. The stomped half of my face feels like an expanding bag of microwave popcorn and I'm not sure how long this arm-tent will hold against the mob. I grab his elbows and haul myself up. He takes one of my hands in his jellyfish hand—squishy palmed and long-fingered, damp from exertion, not nerves—and leads me to the sidewalk outside.

I'm Nik, he says to my left cheek. My most sincere apologies.

Sara, I say. I can tell by the way he hangs on to my hand and his snailing *most* that he's done some serious damage to my face. I cover the swollen cheek with my available palm.

Oh man, you must be in shock, he says. Are you okay?

Okay, I say, but not good. I push his bony shoulder into the brick wall behind him. Why are you wearing shit-kickers in the presence of children?

They're my friend Bruce's. He plays bass in the band. Nik lifts his feet up one at a time as though they're gummed to the sidewalk. He has massive feet, Nik says. I'm more of a Vans guy.

Canvas would be a safer bet.

Nik stares at me like he's watching a baby bird die.

Is it that bad?

It's cute, he says. Like a chipmunk. Nik rests an elbow on top of my backpack and asks if I'm a vagrant.

I guess.

Then you'll come home with me.

His place smells of cumin and compost. I finger his bananas and a mushroom cloud of fruit flies erupts. He peels and cuts a pear for me and makes hot cocoa from scratch. When we finish drinking he holds ice to my cheek with one hand and unbuttons my pants with the other. We tussle like house cats high on butter. I lick his toenails, his scalp. He stays up all night, humming me to sleep and back again.

I wake up alone save for a plate of pancakes soggy with syrup. Nik hasn't left a note or a fork—an obvious invitation to rifle through his drawers. Cutlery mingles with junk in the small drawer below the telephone. Peanut-buttered knives and olive-oiled pasta claws and saliva-ed spoons and glued-shut scissors and wrinkled photographs (Nik with ginger, yoga-panted woman touching tongues, baring teeth, etc.) and one yellow-encrusted fork. I wash off the turmeric-that-is-not-powdery-enough-to-be-turmeric with the most soap-like (bright green, viscous) substance I can find and dig in. Nik makes a decent pancake.

I drift through the apartment in his underwear, comb his carpet with my fingers and wonder about all the long hairs. Where do these red, blonde, brunette, curly, straight-haired girls go after the carpet husking?

The plastic bottles on the rim of his tub are aligned by colour. Turquoise Pert Plus and Ruby Raspberry body wash straddle a dissolving bar of Pears. A kelly-green shower scrunchie pulls up the rear. This guy likes to wash but there is a disturbing lack of soap at his sink. His toilet bowl drips with orange mould and his garbage is padded with yellowed Q-tips. In his defence, he was not expecting company. Bathroom reading materials include a book of crosswords hugged by fountain pen (into grandmotherly mental stimulation), *Explore* (into reading about adventure, not adventure itself), *Thrasher* (poseur—no indication of actual skateboard in apartment), *Spin* (sellout) and no porn (either devout Catholic or not into bathroom masturbation).

I take *Thrasher* to the sofa and read up on how to perfect my kickflip and convince my mom to pave the front yard into a half-pipe. I could adopt Nik's underwear, ford the mighty North Saskatchewan and ride the next rank tin can out of town. Edmonton was not my intended destination. Toronto maybe, Montreal. Come By Chance, Newfoundland. But I am drawn to the disordered order here. Even Nik's dirty laundry is folded into a corner at the foot of his bed. And why the five toothbrushes at attention in an old jam jar next to his sink? Who is this man who would take me in?

The apartment door opens and there stands Nik, looking like a Mormon. Sweater-vested in pleated slacks, he is a wash of grey-toned polyester.

He dips his head and says, Work clothes.

Will you tell me about your God?

I'm glad you stayed.

I have nowhere to go.

I can help you, he says.

I hope he's playing Mormon. I ask him where he works.

Sears. Men's department.

Classy.

In West Edmonton Mall.

Is that good?

They have dolphins.

Like, in captivity?

No, no. Wild mall dolphins.

I don't approve of that.

What, sarcasm?

Animal abuse. I'm vegan.

Nik points to my breakfast plate. You ate eggs.

I assumed they came from happy chickens.

Eggs aren't sentient anyway.

Should we discuss abortion now?

Nik grabs the elastic of his underwear and snaps it against my hip. He takes off his sweater vest and pulls my hair so hard my jaw pops open. He puts his finger in my mouth. It tastes like bus pole. Salt and metal and gum residue. I bite it to keep it clear of my flesh. We buckle our knees and he undoes his belt, huffing like a bear.

Nik gets me a job behind the jewellery counter at Sears. I shadow Jenna. She's a six-foot-tall blonde with cleavage so ripe I want to sleep in it. She tells me there's no dress code but I can't wear anything ironic or unravelled. And I must always arrive sock-footed. I tell Jenna people can't see my feet but she says they'll know.

From my vantage point in Jenna's shadow, to properly perform at this job, one must flip the phone-cord bracelet of keys around and around one's wrist, angle the customer mirror toward oneself and fix one's hair in a cradle-palmed, poofing action as though stuffing clouds into an at-capacity sky, and invent reasons to call security so that, once a uniformed man arrives, one can lean over the counter, squeeze one's breasts with upper arms and sarcastically ask after his girlfriend. Does Nik think these tasks fit within the purview of my repertoire?

Jenna requests that I clean the glass counter while she files her nails. I request that she not file her nails over my lunch bag.

Why?

You're getting bits of nail on my apple.

Jenna leans over my lunch. I don't see any bits, she says.

What do you think comes off when you file?

Nothing comes off. It's shaping.

How do you think it shapes?

Jenna whips her file up like a conductor's baton. With this, she says.

I rescue my apple and wander the store in search of Nik. There he is, tucked between Major Appliances and Ladies' Handbags, tugging at ties on a rung to align their tips. I slurp apple and watch from behind a rack of women's all-weather coats. Nik folds sweaters and arranges them by size, he picks at bits of brown crud on the wall with his thumbnail, he stops to stare at the ceiling, pockets his hands and taps his toes. And when a wizened candy cane of an older gentleman pulls at his sleeve, Nik startles and slowly shifts his attention like a little boy drawn from a daydream.

There's a new dispenser in town. Liquid hand soap, meet Nik's bathroom sink. His kitchen counter is now a legume spa. A sprout incubator. The game we play: Who is Sara? He knows I arrived on a bus from Victoria. I wear a size-seven Dr. Marten. He knows I like being kissed on the mole under my left armpit. I have a postcard from my dad in the top of my backpack and the only thing I'll say about it is *maybe*. Is he travelling? Maybe. Are you looking for him? Maybe. Does he know you're here? Maybe. I'm on the floor in Nik's underwear, wrapped in near-naked Nik.

Why are you here? he says.

Because you invited me.

I mean Edmonton.

I was so done with the bus at Edmonton.

Why the bus?

Faster than walking.

Why leave?

Why stay?

Nik looks all concerned on his hands and knees, his Sears-issue lanyard dangling in tandem with his balls.

It's better here, I say.

Nik mouths my cheek, sucks like a child indulging in bathwater from a sponge. I break the seal, burrow my head into his stomach and proclaim love to his navel.

The next day at the jewellery counter, there's an old lady jonesing for earrings. She is a pastel rump roast, sectioned by the elastic of her undergarments. A tray of our finest, reminiscent of a dental office treasure trove, does not satisfy. I suggest a necklace instead.

Earrings, dear, she says loud and slow like I'm deaf or mentally infirm, fingers jiggling her lobes.

Why did you call me dear? Do I remind you of your granddaughter or do you like to patronize those who serve you?

She looks to both sides, fingers still cleaved to lobe as though escorting her head. Is there someone else who could help me?

Jenna's the affable one but she's on break.

Do you have a manager, dear?

There you go again calling me dear.

My manager, Doreen, weaves toward Jewellery through racks of wan polyester shirts, pinching them at the shoulders so they properly droop from their hangers. I shout, Will that be on your Sears card today? but the lady snaps her waistband with her thumbs and storms off. I give Doreen a thumbs-up and she veers toward Ladies' Swimwear.

Nik eats eggs for breakfast. Every morning, rivulets of yolk drip from the corners of his carnivorous mouth. He's a chick murderer. Jack the Ripper. He could be fattening me up on tofu and coconut milk in order to one day knock me out with that lone, rolling barbell under his bed, pin me by the hair to the back of his closet with the tips of his razor-sharp cross-country ski poles and gnaw at me bit by bit. He spirals a crust of bread around his plate until it is saturated with yolk, then curls it onto his long, thin eel tongue. And his eyes, so small and dark, at times impenetrable as a rodent's and other times black-hole open. He traces a finger above his eyebrows and around his ear, tucking a phantom lock. I ask if he used to have long hair and he nods. My stomach tightens. He lived before me. Of course he did. But how dare he?

Would you eat a human? I say.

What?

Meat is meat.

Don't be one of *those* vegans.

What if we were shipwrecked on a desert island?

I'd eat coconuts and sand.

What if the power went out and we were trapped here for days?

Then I'd eat you.

I stomp my little heel on his big, hairy hobbit toes. Nik, why did you ask me here?

You were cute and I felt bad for stepping on you.

What about now?

You're still cute. He holds the back of my neck like a beer can and smears his yolky tongue across my cheek. You do taste good, he says.

Nik, really.

Clean hands, good sex.

Anyone can buy soap.

Not the lavender, turmeric, blood-of-a-rowan-tree kind.

Nik?

Living with you is like doing a crossword with made-up words.

Every Wednesday night, Nik's friend Bruce knocks at the door, his head cloaked in black hoodie. Grim Reaper with DVD in hand. Nik worships Bruce. Bruce is passable. He makes killer vegan popcorn and is aware of Engevita yeast. Nik thought it was an infection. When Bruce is around, Nik smokes hand-rolled cigarettes like joints, between his thumb and pointer finger. He calls me *Babe* and doesn't do the dishes. Insensitive-badass Nik would be comical if he weren't mine. I call him *Sugar* and I don't do the dishes either. We'll see who folds first. I could go ages on dirty dishes, he has no idea.

Tonight, when the movie's over, Bruce looks at me and says, *Zoolander* made you cry?

I don't like endings, I say.

He jerks his hands like he's touched a hot stove and says, Sen-si-tive.

I hate Bruce.

—

The phone rings an octave higher than the status quo. It's Nik's mother. This creature normally calls on Sundays. Nik's end of the conversation is all: Good. Yeah. Sorry. Yeah.

Then he's quiet for a while.

Yeah. Okay. No, no. I understand. Yeah, okay. No, no. Sure. Of course. Two-thirty. It's no problem. Happy to help.

When he hangs up he asks how I feel about kids.

Baby goats?

My little stepsister.

Does she have child eyes that can see through you?

She can see like a normal person.

Will she pick her nose and wipe it in my hair?

She's done that like once.

Nik's mom arrives with a ragamuffin in a sundress. The girl is wedged between her mother's legs wearing heart-shaped sunglasses and pink lip gloss, her sloppy French braid the aftermath of a mother-daughter tug-of-war. I envy her, then the feeling passes.

Nik's mom looks at me and says, What happened to Samantha?

Nik says, I've been meaning to. This is—

The flavour of the month, she says.

I say, Hey, I'm Rocky Road. Call me Sara.

The ragamuffin says, I have a doll named Sara but Mom doesn't like her because she has blue hair.

I used to have blue hair.

Nik's mom stretches her lips and extends an abnormally large hand. I'm Linda, she says. I'm sure Nik hasn't mentioned me.

I shake her middle finger and say, I haven't mentioned my mom either. Mostly 'cause she's a lunatic.

Linda says, Well, and stares at us a while. She crosses her arms and separates her lips aquatically. Nik reminds her she needed to do something important like show a house on Connaught Drive.

Linda looks at Nik and says, You'll be with her the whole time? You're not going to leave her with—

Yes, Nik says.

Nik's stepsister's name is Marie. Like Marie Antoinette, says the girl. Let them eat cake. Nik tells me he taught her that. Queen Marie squats on the carpet, her knees rolling into each other. Got any toys? she says.

I roll an orange toward her toes and say, Ball.

Nik says, She's not two.

I light up Nik's hand-rolled and hold it toward her. Cigarette? Nik suggests we go for a walk.

L'Autrichienne holds onto each of our hands and swings between us singing one-two-three whee. We walk down Whyte Avenue and point things out. Look, a rainbow, says Nik. Look, a forgotten soul, I say. Nik grins over Marie's head, displays the horse-perfect teeth of someone whose parents had a dental plan.

We bump into Bruce outside Blackbyrd Myoozik and he and Nik have an intense conversation about Bruce's amp. Is it loud/large/portable enough? Can he afford to buy a new one? Can he afford not to? Nik leans his head against the store window and reaches for Bruce's cigarette with thumb and pointer. Nik's olive-green Army & Navy pants are two inches too short and the holes in his socks rise above the tops of his shoes. Pinned to his jacket, a fake carnation a homeless guy traded him for a dollar. He looks so smitten. I admire, distrust, resent his capacity to love.

Marie and I fold ourselves onto the sidewalk, cross-legged—Marie with a little girl's disregard for what's going on with her panties. She rests her head on my arm.

You're pretty, she says. I like you. Marie pulls a sparkly pink slipper off her right foot. Do you like my shoes?

They're a bit shiny.

Mom got them for me 'cause I cleaned my room. Like Cinderella.

Marie holds the shoe under my nose because the closer something is to your face, the better you see it. It smells like marshmallows. Marshmallows and bum. I take Queen Marie's shoe and throw it into a mud puddle. Nik jumps to Marie's side as though the splash was a gunshot.

What? he says. Why?

Who, where, when? I say.

Nik gropes for the shoe but doesn't look me in the eye. Bruce calls me a wack job but Marie enjoys a wet foot.

Do it to the other one, she squeals.

We return home to Nik's mom, smoking on the hood of her Lexus. Marie is brown-footed and drippy-shoed.

What did you do to her? Nik's mom says.

We went for a walk, Nik says.

Through a lake?

Mud puddle.

How?

Kids. Nik shakes his head and offers a palm to the sky.

Nik's mom bites her lips closed and breathes out her nose, like a flameless dragon. Marie pokes a finger into the hole at the knee of my leggings. Nik's mom tugs at her other hand, says, It's time to go.

Marie rips my hole a little more. You're invited to my birth-day party.

When is it?

Dunno.

Apparently, Sears employees are not allowed to borrow from the till. Not even a fiver to buy a soyaccino on break. Apparently, Big Brother is watching. Nik convinces them not to press charges. He uses the word *free-spirited*.

Jenna ringlets her hair with her fingers and says, This is supposed to be a scent-free environment but I get a strong patchouli smell from Sara.

I say, At least I look professional at work. You don't see Jenna in a sweater vest, do you?

Doreen says to Nik and Jenna, She never promotes the Sears card.

Nik says, Sara has different ideas about rules.

And I don't care anymore about this bauble-hawking, grumpy grandma–appeasing job because Nik understands a part of me I've never put into words.

Everything in the apartment likes Nik more than me. The TV remote is unresponsive. The faucets geyser. The fridge makes loud, indigestive noises. I cook cauldrons of chickpeas and tamaried tofu under endive cover. I am vegan Martha. Shall we craft?

Nik arrives home to a bouquet of newsprint tulips. Jean Chrétien and George W. in petalled embrace. Market numbers fraternizing with one-day sales and masking tape. I've left him a trail of newsprint petals, dyed romance-red with a light glossing of beet juice and ketchup. For hours now, I've awaited him in bed wearing nothing but a spoonful of curry on my chest. A third, turmeric breast. Arms above my head, hair spread. Burning yellow heart.

Nik enters and says, It looks like a cat ralphed on you.

Eat it.

It's been a long day, Sara.

Take the curry.

Nik scoops the glob of curry into his palm, stares at it.

Eat it?

Sara.

He says my name in his not-now voice. With a never-ending second *a*. The same voice he uses when I channel surf during an Oilers game or ask him to sing "Wind Beneath My Wings" at one of our fruit-fly funerals.

I roll away from him.

Sara?

I make extravagant love to my pillow and don't look at Nik once, though he watches the entire production. Nik's pillow. It's Nik's pillow.

I'm disgracefully scattered all over this apartment. Safety pins in the ficus, toothbrush atop the mirror, incense under the mattress. My straight browns have dominion over the carpet by force of number. I've been here a few months and Nik's cut me a key but hasn't bequeathed me any space. Not his sock drawer, a corner of closet, the bathtub. Will he even miss me? He claims he loves me but every morning, there he is again with the eggs. And what *did* happen to Samantha?

I fill my backpack, turtle up and leave. The infamous princess-shoe mud puddle outside Blackbyrd Myoozik is now dry enough to squat in, and so I do. Window shoppers, Americano hunters and bus catchers throw coins at me, tell me to get a job. In the trash nearby I find a pizza box and a pen on its deathbed, hemorrhaging ink. I create a sign to prop up against my pack: *Victoria or Bust*. The stream of cash slows. Clearly Edmontonians resent the western migration of their free spirits.

Once four nickel-and-dime dollars accumulate between my legs, I head to the neo-hippie pizza parlour for a slice of Vegan Chick-Peazza. I eat with record-breaking unspeed, crumb by crumb. Where to now? A small, insistent part of me votes for an attention-getting non-runaway scenario.

My server, Chuck, asks if I'd like another slice.

Would you like me to pay for it?

Yes.

Then no.

Chuck returns to his station behind the till and alternates between reading the free weekly and staring at me. Crumb by crumb, Chuck. Crumb by crumb. We repeat this conversation once an hour. It becomes our thing, Chuck and I. When the new server arrives at the end of his shift he debriefs her. He says, She's still technically eating. And drinking. Yes, water.

Nik walks outside the parlour window. Hands in pockets, shoulders drawn to ears, winged elbows. He assumes this stance when mulling over puzzles like what to do Friday night or where, oh where his Sara has gone. He stops to tie an errant shoelace.

I press my cheek to the glass. Maybe she's in here, I say.

Nik turns to peek inside.

Maybe she's in here.

He waves.

I wave.

Nik enters, grabs hold of my table from underneath, then snaps his hands back into his pockets, like he'd momentarily forgotten that the number one gum-wad habitat is a table's underbelly.

Why are you here? he says.

Why are you here?

Because you're here.

Here we are.

I was worried.

You haven't even given me a toothbrush jar, I say.

Nik sighs and fingers a crumb labyrinth on my plate. I extend my pointer and middle and tug at the hem of his shirt. I fit my other pointer into his navel.

Sorry about the curry, he says.

It's not for everyone.

I'm sorry I ate it all when I got home and you weren't there.

Was it dahlectable?

Nik shakes his head. Currific.

I knew you'd korma-round.

Nik takes hold of my finger, still stuck in his remarkably lint-free navel. He nods at my booth. Room in there for me?

What to Expect

Life, as It Was, with Twinges of Dissatisfaction

The night I was no longer enough, Nik and I followed a stray cat down fifteen alleys and into a hole in the wall of the Royal Bank on Whyte Avenue. We named him Barney due to his girth, purple tinge and cartoonish, prehistoric amble. He snugged himself into the hole until he was flush with the bricks and purred himself to sleep.

Nik lay a hand on Barney's vibrating chest. We should have a baby, he said. Isn't it great to watch something sleep?

You can watch me sleep.

You're not little.

I am so little.

Not little enough.

And so began the *enough*s. Two was not family enough. Watering and performing ABBA hits for our houseplants was not nurturing enough. Compiling an ethnography of the neighbourhood cats was not important enough.

Back at home, Nik yanked the book from my hand mid-sentence. He was trying to be passionate. Domino the salt and pepper shakers, abolish the lentil casserole, let it rain silverware, *I must have you on the countertop right now* passionate. But we don't do that. Beds are so comfortable.

Nik grabbed my ponytail and pulled me toward him. This used to drive me crazy but now it only drives me crazy. It seemed important though, so I didn't say, *Do you want me to end up one of those patchy-scalped women who eat whole chickens from the deli and do crosswords at the seniors' centre while slowly dying alone?* He threw me to the bed, lifted my skirt and pulled down my panties with one finger hooked into the crotch.

No condom, he said. Let's make a baby.

He kept saying it as he wrung out my thighs and poked me from the back and tried and tried and finally flipped me over and missionaried me.

~~ARE YOU PREGNANT?~~ *Are You About to Grow a Six-to-Eight Pound Immeasurable Weight?*

Nik inspected the bathroom garbage for menstrual paraphernalia daily. He thought I didn't notice, but I noticed. I saw him fingering my floss. I smothered maxi pads in barbecue sauce and planted them around the apartment. Kitchen garbage, bathroom garbage, under his pillow. I left a ketchuped tampon on his nightstand and he held it to me, limp like the last cold, soggy pub fry you know you shouldn't eat but you do because you paid for the whole basket and you might be hungry later. He said *Sara* the way he does now. The way he inflates the last *a* with balloons of disappointment.

Yes?

Too bad you're on the rag constantly.

Crazy, right?

Almost unnatural.

Like immaculate conception but the opposite.

Sara, he says again with the *a*.

Yes?

Do you not want a baby anymore?

Did I want a baby?

Should we look for cats?

We hunted for Ombre. Sleek and black, the pantheriest feline in the hood. An enigma, mostly. But a sucker for smoked salmon. Ombre hung out between Old Strathcona's gay/cougar dance bar, the Purple Onion, and Raj Pannu's office next to it. Raj was one of Alberta's only New Democrat MLAs. He wore a T-shirt that said *Raj Against the Machine* when out and about. Though they say kids these days don't vote, I think the support of the angry-alternatives swung it for him last election.

It was nine o'clock so the only people outside the Onion were a couple of eager fourteen-year-old girls who'd just acquired fake IDs from some thirty-five-year-old perv named Joey with surprisingly clean hair and yellow fingers that smelled of their dad's old pipe collection. Probably. When the door of the bar opened and the George Michael drifted out, they wiggled their hips and giggled, then stopped as soon as the door closed like it was a game of freeze tag.

A fierce black tail curled out from the bike racks by the PO's door. Ombre. The girls got to him first with their lip-glossed fingers and their *Heeeeere kitty*s. Ombre squeezed between the buildings where the girls and their strawberry-scented fingers couldn't reach. He rubbed his back on Raj's side. Leaned to the left. I opened the salmon.

I gurgled his name throatily, like I was horking a phlegm wad.

Ombre turned his head. Sniffed. Slunk over. He smelled the salmon, licked the salmon, slunk away. Sidled up to Chez Pannu and didn't look back.

You got the wrong stuff, I said.

You picked it out.

You wanted to go to the IGA.

No I didn't.

It's closest to our place.

So it's my fault we live where we do?

It's your apartment.

Sara? Are you pregnant?

I sat down on the sidewalk a few concrete slabs down from the fourteen-year-old girls. Legs outstretched, they pulled their toes toward themselves like two little mousetraps.

I shook my head and told Nik my period's on hiatus.

Nik put his hand on my stomach and cupped the little zygote.

~~YOUR PREGNANCY LIFESTYLE~~

You Have Too Many Sharp Edges

In all the movies I'd seen about babies, the main-character mother has a sidekick momma. The sidekick momma is more together— she's married and she owns a house with a fence and she has an actual room for the baby full of soft-hued, big-eyed items. The main-character mother is single and got knocked up one wild night at the bar while celebrating the defence of her master's thesis on the male gaze and subordination of the female body and she didn't use a condom because she thought it would be too ironic to be impregnated that night. I had no sidekick momma.

All I had was Nik. He was a fine sidekick. He kept me away from peroxide and kitty litter and he ground folic acid into my morning peanut butter. But he was no momma.

I noticed one of the servers at Cafe Mosaics was protruding as of late. Wearing a lot of empire waistlines. Little extra pancake under the jaw. I ordered the vegan huevos rancheros and stared her down. She was in jeans with a little tummy that peeked through when she reached up for plates and condiments. Her tummy looked unnaturally firm and her waistband was elasticized. Definitely preggers. When she refilled my coffee cup I asked how far along she was.

Not done 'til four, she said.

This is your fourth child? I was so bold as to point directly at her expanding navel.

What?

Your baby?

Oh. How did you...

We should be pregnant together.

Um.

Maybe we could assemble a frustrating crib or go to pregnacize.

Sidekick Momma's smile became tight and toothy like a french-fry basket. How's the huevos?

So good.

In a few weeks, one look at that and you'll ralph.

Sidekick Momma left and stayed in the back with the cook while I finished off what was looking more and more like a pile of vomit. I stayed a while, sipping coffee and exchanging pleasantries with my fellow patrons (*Grainy coffee today. Isn't Patsy Cline timeless? Whatcha writing?*) but Sidekick Momma never returned to my table. After half an hour, the cook came out and asked me to pay my bill and leave because a line was forming. I would be back.

In the movies, the main-character mother also has an overbearing mother who makes passive-aggressive remarks about her daughter's lack of husband and tries to fix her up with anyone in possession of a penis and a regular paycheque. It will end up being the overbearing mother's gay hairdresser and they'll all have a good laugh over that one.

That night, Nik made the first in a series of taste-free dinners save for the ginger to stave off my morning sickness. Whenever he was home, he kept a protective hand trained on my lower abdomen as though my amniotic fluid wasn't cushion enough.

Nik, I have no ladies.

You have me.

I need someone who's pushed a creature from her vagina.

Nik choked on ginger brown rice. Birth canal.

Vagina.

Stop it. What about my mom?

Your mom's a realtor.

She's birthed.

She wears shoulder pads.

Your mother?

Your mom's pretty nurturing, actually.

Sara, you should call your mom.

Remember that time your mom made you a birthday cake... like a month after your birthday?

That's not fair. My mom's dyslexic.

I've been gone four years. My mother's probably too drunk to remember me.

Call your mom.

Hello? ... Who is this? ... What is 780? ... Where is that? ... If
you're one of those Ethiopian Princes... I'm no idiot.

~~THE FIRST MONTH~~ *You Can't Barf It Out*

I was sitting in a yellow patch of grass against the chain-link
fence of the Boo Radley house at the bus stop on 109th Street—
home to Fluffy Fran and Cat Bjelland and no humans visible to
the naked eye—when it hit me that I was pregnant. I was going
to give birth to a human being and I was going to be a mother.
And what if I was my mother? Nik got off the bus and found
me, green-faced, fingers woven into Fran's fluff, staring at the
cars, cars, cars driving by at the same pace. He crouched down.
His slacks rose to mid-calf. That's what he wore to work. Slacks.
Pants were for pleasure. His grey socks stopped above ankle
where they were met with hair, hair, hair all in a mess of assertion,
each one poking out to a more fruitful beyond-slack existence.
His sweater vest matched his socks exactly, but his slacks not so
exactly. Nik didn't understand monochromatic clashing. He said
grey is grey is grey.

Sara? he said, for maybe the fifth time.

I can't take care of a baby.

I can.

Are you saying I can't?

No. You said that. You did.

You said.

I meant I'll help you.

Help?

Together.

Nik took my hand and walked me home. During those three hundred steps, everything about him—his long thin fingers, the way they wrapped around mine like ivy, his steady job, his slacks, his hair slicked to one side in order to mimic his customers, in order to bring himself down to their Tim Hortons coffee–drinking, *Edmonton Sun*–reading, Oilers season ticket-holding level so they'd buy polyester products from him, the way he rinsed it when he got home but didn't shampoo so it would be easier to slick the next morning—everything that made him seem as though he'd be the man most likely to father my children— made me want to spew voluminous chunks.

Hello? ... Is this the same number as before? ... Are you the guy
I met at Logan's? ... Clive?

~~THE SECOND MONTH~~ *You Might Regret This*

There was ample rotundity at Kinsmen Spray Park. Like the whole city had procreated and all the pregnant ladies were gathered at the local watering hole. Expectant candy ravers with overextended tube tops, exposed navels and pacifiers laced with ecstasy. Yuppies warming buns in the oven in stiletto heels. Gravid granolas wrapped in calm presence and elasticized hemp. I sat next to a granola at the side of the paddling pool and dipped my toes in the chlorinated urine. I webbed my hands on the concrete beside me so our fingers almost touched. The granola didn't look over at me. I arched my back so she would notice my blossoming embryo and know we were compatriots. Still, she didn't look over. A couple of yuppie preggers chatted behind us. *When are you due? Are you using a midwife? God, no. Scheduled*

C-section. Are you taking parental leave? Do you have your name in at a daycare? Is there a bathroom around here? One that's not for hook-ups?

The granola groaned, wet her belly, then got up and barefooted away. She was replaced by a toddler whose swim diaper squelched when she stumbled onto my legs. Her mother swooped in and grabbed her by the armpits, apologizing the way mothers do to non-mothers.

I'm *so* sorry. Emma, you got that lady all wet.

If I were a mother she would've shaken her head and said, *Kids.* I stayed at the spray park with my toes underwater until the sun lowered and the population went full cycle from splashing families to picnicking lovers to shuffling, lone men.

When I returned home, Nik's eyes had grown an inch closer to one another. He sat at the kitchen table in an upright fetal position aimed at the living room. I could smell his mother. Rusty metal with a hint of lemon. His little stepsister Marie, too. Grape cough syrup and flip-flops after a day at the beach. A series of *don't*s emanated from the living room. *Don't bounce on the sofa, don't rub your hair on the cushion, don't touch your bum in public.* I smudged the door shut and flattened myself to the wall. Nik made no sign that he noticed me. I crouched low, crossed right leg over left down the hall.

Nik owled his head toward me. I thought you'd be here when I got home from work.

I was observing women-with-child.

Nik blinked, but remained otherwise stationary. I asked my mom over, he said. With child.

Marie skipped into the hall, bunned and swaddled in pink spandex, crucifix arms, toes lifting to opposite knees, singing, And one and two and three and four.

How's it hanging, Marie?

Marie dug her hands under my shirt and squished around the fetus. I'm going to be an auntie. Babybabybaby.

Nik's mom strode over, heel-toe, heel-toe in a pair of sand-coloured clogs. No doubt an attempt to fit in with the ballet mother crowd, distinguishable from the stage mother crowd by the duck-like spread and bunioned state of their feet. She smacked at Marie's fingers.

Don't hurt the baby. Then she said, Well. Congratulations. Her timbre rose and fell with each syllable like a voicemail robot. I brought over some of my old maternity clothes. She gestured to a garbage bag hunched by the apartment door. She squeezed the bag at its middle. It vomited trails of faux denim tents and stretchy stomach inserts from its thin, plastic lips. Then she said, You won't want to wear them in public, of course. Nik's mom pushed Marie away with a straight-armed hand to her ribcage and leaned into my face. Sara, she said. You might regret this now, but you're not alone. She lowered her arm, pulled Marie toward her by the hand and told her they needed to get to ballet class.

But I'm visiting the baby.

Marie. Now.

Marie let go of my stomach and one-and-two'ed out, Nik's mom clip-clopping behind.

How do I access this coterie of regret?

Hello? ... Ha-Lo?

Hi.

Who is this?

I'm pregnant.

This isn't a help line.

I know.

Why are you calling me?

You have kids?

Two daughters.

That's why.

You sound like… Sara?

~~THE THIRD MONTH~~
Don't Lose Your Lunch or Your Sperm Source

On Saturday mornings, Nik always woke up early, watered the plants, sang a little "Super Trouper" for the droopy ficus, and brought me oatmeal in bed. He was bent over, looking for his slippers or maybe checking out the stray hairs under the bed when I said, Don't go.

Hmm?

Don't go. I pulled at his waist. Don't go. I bit his sleep-sticky thigh. Stay in bed. I looked up at him. He said *Sara* the way he does. The way he inflates the last *a* with helium so it can float away. He turned to me and filled my navel with tongue. He spread a bat-wing hand between my shoulder blades and tapered it down my spine until it was one middle finger on my tailbone. One middle finger up my bum and one tongue spread over my thighs.

Don't go, don't go, don't.

Nik moved his finger and I said, Stop.

He didn't stop and again, I said, Stop.

Don't stop?

Stop. Your finger. The baby.

It won't touch the baby.

You'll get it dirty.

Sara, he said, the *a* drooping.

Wash your finger.

Fine.

Nik left the room and ran the tap for a few seconds. He came back twenty minutes later carrying a bowl of oatmeal with extra banana. I don't know if he ever washed his finger. Like, with soap.

Sorry, I said. It's just.

Yeah. No. Cleanliness. The baby.

My bum. And then up my—

Birth canal. Yup.

E. coli and stuff.

Nik smiled not a real smile but a curling of his lips underneath all his teeth and raising of his eyebrows. He slapped my thigh like a coach. I'm going for a run, he said and he left the apartment in his pyjama bottoms and slippers.

I had not seen Nik run in the four years I'd known him. I'd seen him trot after Marie with a dropped mitten. I'd seen him canter after a missed bus. But no running.

I donned Nik's mother's extra-wide avocado A-line mini dress even though my stomach was no bigger than it would be had I eaten too much dark chocolate, and I scoured the neighbourhood for Nik. I intended to scour. What I really did was purr at a few felines and hover near the dumpster behind Cafe Mosaics.

When Sidekick Momma emerged from the kitchen door, the backs of my thighs were perforated from the asphalt and I couldn't move. She leaned against the dumpster and lit a smoke.

You're that crazy pregnant girl, she said.

I nodded.

She held up her cigarette. I have one a day, she said. For the baby. You want?

I reached out two fingers.

Still eating huevos?

I have an aversion to vegan cheez. And tamari and molasses.

It's alfredo sauce for me.

And candy canes.

Mangoes.

Who's the dad? I pointed to her stomach.

The baby? I think it's Dan. The cook inside. How about you?

Nik. My... I guess he's my boyfriend.

Complicated?

Too simple. I left home when I was eighteen and ended up here. He's the first person I met.

Sounds nice.

He leaves toothpaste goo everywhere and he eats runny eggs, but yeah.

You been together long?

Four years.

Wow. Can't imagine that.

I can't imagine not-Nik.

I rolled onto my front and stood up. I put out my cigarette and brushed the tar bits from my dress, thanked Sidekick Momma for the smoke.

I'm Jenny, she said.

Sara.

Come back sometime. We'll have a coffee.

I skipped home, sure I would find Nik, pyjama'd and listless. I would jump in his lap and tell him he could spread my anal residue anywhere he damn well pleased. But he wasn't home. No note, no yolky breakfast plate. Not-Nik.

Hello? ... You again? ... Back to heavy breathing? ... Sara, is it you? ... How's the baby?

He's gone.

Your baby?

My Nik.

Your what?

The father.

Where are you? ... Sara? ... Sara?

~~THE FOURTH MONTH~~ *A Baby by Any Other Name*

The first day of not-Nik, I stayed in bed until three p.m. I telepathically willed nourishment to join me. A parade of pickles, a tortilla trek. The refrigerator did not comply. Four p.m. found me on the couch, catatonic with chips. I slept there and awoke the next day with greased-salt stubble.

Nik arrived a few hours later, flopped next to me and sighed as though he'd just had a really long shift at work.

How was your run?

He swept the crumbs off my face with his palm and wiped it on his slacks, which weren't the pyjamas he left home in.

Where've you been?

My mom's. I'm sorry.

It's okay. You're back now.

About the baby. You weren't ready.

I pressed my greasy face into his slacks, between his thighs. I turned my head up and said, Is anyone ever ready?

Nik held my head and squeezed my earlobe between his thumb and first finger. He said, Maybe not.

We sat there until his next shift at Sears. He went to the kitchen and scooped a spoonful of peanut butter for himself. He returned to the couch, a spooned brown glob in hand. I gotta go to work, he said. He kissed me. Peanut butter and tongue and Nik, Nik, Nik. The spoon was fully nested in my hair. I could feel the weight of it when I shifted my head.

I want you, he said, his hand up his mom's dress.

I want you too. I want your baby.

Nik corked my crotch with his thumb. He stayed there, looking at me, above me. Before the baby, he'd been so easy to read. He loved everything that loved him back. He helped everything that needed help. Now he had a sinister look in his eyes, like he was trying to plug the baby's air hole. But then he removed his thumb, he sucked it and he said, What about Juniper?

We could call her June bug.

Or Juni. But we'd pronounce it Yuni to be pretentious.

First day of kindergarten.

Uh, that's Yuniper.

*J*s are so pedestrian.

Nik took the spoon out of my hair and told me to take a shower. He said he'd see me later and it took all the faith I had to not ask if he would ever come back.

This is Gwen. I don't want to talk to you right now. *Beep.*

Hi. It's me. He came back. I thought you might want to know.

I'm in Edmonton. You asked, so.

~~THE FIFTH MONTH~~ *Do/a the Right Thing*

Come October, I was permanently cloaked in avocado A-line. The little honeydew under my ribs was coming to life. Like popping corn. Nik would put his ear to my belly and say he felt it.

That was indigestion.

Now?

Gas.

Now?

Yeah. A kick.

I resided at a table for one in the back corner of Cafe Mosaics on Wednesday afternoons when the boss took off. Jenny would put up the CLOSED sign and take her break. We'd have a cigarette and bottomless coffee and, if he was feeling paternal, Dan fried some tofu to feed our little soybeans. We talked about baby names and men. Mostly I said things and she told me she had it worse. I'd tell her my back was killing me and she'd say, *Wait 'til you're eight months pregnant.* I'd tell her that Nik refused to read me a bedtime story the night before and she'd say, *Dan had full sex with some Princess Leia–bunned sixteen-year-old on the stovetop yesterday at close while I mopped the café.* Jenny wasn't my housed and fenced sidekick momma. We were the blind leading the blind.

I found this great doula, Jenny said.

Is that like a skort?

Like a birth assistant.

Sounded like clothes.

She's practically a Viking.

Is that helpful?

She blew up an entire exercise ball with her mouth.

She must give amazing head.

Great. Now Dan's gonna hit on her while I push this football out.

Should I get one?

You can use mine when I'm done with her.

Like a skort.

A Norwegian Forest cat poked her head into the hall when I opened our apartment door. She squinted at me through her rusty fluff. Was this Porcupine, who held court inside the tire ladder at the Garneau School playground? Porcupine was chubbier, mangier, and her coat was juice-box sticky and perpetually scattered with sandwich crumbs. No, this grimalkin was unknown. Nik rounded the kitchen corner on all fours, his stretched-out, heel-holed socks trailed a few inches behind him.

I haven't named her yet. I knew you'd want to, he said.

Who is it?

She's from the SPCA.

She's ours?

Baby practice.

Oh.

You hate her. She's too fluffy.

No.

Not scruffy enough.

Like Porcupine. But not.

You only like the strays.

You're no different.

I bought this cat.

Did you know I wanted to go all the way to Montreal? But I only made it here.

Nik picked up the cat and held her level with his face. He said, Montreal is only a city.

And I'm only a stray.

That makes no sense.

I sat on the floor at Nik's knees. The avocado A-line now barely covered my rear. I spread my fingers and raked them across the carpet toward myself. You only want to gather family, I said.

Why is that bad? Nik sat down in front of me. He pulled up his shapeless socks, which immediately sagged back down, and pressed his feet into my feet so that we made a diamond, hermetically sealed by our foot sweat, like we were stretching each other in gym class. A little pen for the cat. Nik didn't look at me. He looked at his fingers, pressed into the floor in front of his crotch. I knew every cuticle, every ridge of those knuckles.

It's not bad. It's foreign, I said. I bent my knees and entered his half of the diamond. I poked the tip of my nose into his ear and whispered, Can we name her Asslan?

She is pretty royal.

Yet, ours.

Sara.

Hey.

So you're in Edmonton?

Yup.

Why?

Pit stop.

Why don't you come back to Victoria?

Was I an accident?

Sort of. Yes.

Did you want me?

Sure.

Do you regret having me?

What else would I have done with myself?

You could've gone to Montreal.

Could've done a lot of things.

On karaoke night at the Onion, Jenny and I bellied through the crowd. Baby shower, comin' through, she yelled. Nik, Dan and Jackie the doula trailed behind, Nik stating our pregnancies in apologetic tones and Dan circling a pointer finger around his temple. Nik wondered if dancing at a gay/cougar bar was what you were supposed to do at a baby shower but I told him if women can eat coconut-rimmed frozen bananas and play ring the penis at a stagette why do we have to eat cucumber sandwiches and play pin the diaper on the baby? I even brought a baby doll I found in a free box so we could volley it to each other and squeal at it like bachelorettes with plastic penises.

We congregated at a round table overlooking the dance floor. Lady Superpregs, Lady of the Third Trimester, Lady of the Large Lungs, the chivalrous Sir Nik Protector of the Belly and Sir Dan of the Wandering Eye. Anytime someone looked at Jenny the wrong way, or any way at all, she'd say something like, *My fetus belongs to me*, or, *Are you going to care this much about my kid once it's out?* This allowed us a wide circumference in which to dance.

A bare-chested diminutive strawberry blond with robin's nests of pit hair took to the mic to sing Madonna. He had so mastered the throaty scratch and elbows-magnetized-behind-his-back tit jiggle during "Papa Don't Preach," Jenny belly-blocked anyone else who attempted to take the stage. Soon, we were his backup. We slicked our hair into buns with beer and chipotle mayo, painted ourselves with Jackie's Erik the Red lipstick and got our little man to sing some Robert Palmer.

During our gyrating humpy-train "Simply Irresistible" dance, Jenny wet the floor. At first I thought she'd whacked our friend's beer off its stool while exuberantly arm circling but then I noticed her pants had darkened from rose to fuchsia.

Jackie sprinted over to Jenny before you could dip an oar into her body of amniotic fluid. She snaked Jenny's arm around her neck, yelled, *Dan!* and marched the two of them out of the bar.

I looked at Nik. He looked at me. I shrugged and said, What do we do?

He flicked a sugar packet. What's the protocol?

Send baby's breath?

Make her a casserole.

Buy cigars.

Sara? I haven't spoken to you this much in your life.

My friend had a baby.

Hmm.

Did you have friends with babies?

I had nobody.

Dad?

Snort.

Forget it.

Sorry.

I don't know why I even.

Don't hang up.

How's Meg?

Your sister takes care of me.

Sorry.

Forget it.

Post-baby Jenny was absolutely no fun. Her eyelids drooped like turkey wattle, she couldn't focus on people or conversation and she was obsessed with her nipples. Her areole. She spoke a different language. *Nipple latch, swaddle, self-soothe, co-sleep.*

I'd never been to her place so I brought a steaming dish of lentils and brown rice to the café. Dan told me where I could find her. I handed him a cigar and he threw it in with the breakfast links.

Jenny's place was a mish of dissatisfied woman (Rosie the Riveter poster, fishnet stockings, hair in every drain, assortment of herbal teas) toothed into a mash of barely there man (toilet seat in upright position, signed Messier poster, studded collar, overwhelming condom selection). She sat with a baby atop a half-lifesaver cushion around her waist. He slept with her nipple attached to his top lip. Every few seconds, his head would jerk backward thus dislodging lip from nipple and he lunged at her breast, bobbed his head until he made areolar contact and sucked ferociously. His arm remained above his head throughout, as though sunbathing. Jenny's head was tilted so far back it looked like the top of her neck was the entrance to a hinged cookie jar.

Hey Jenny? Jenny.

Snore, snort.

Jenny.

Oh, hey Sara.

Hey.

Snore.

Jenny.

Oh my God. Will you take this thing off my nipple so I can smack myself?

Jenny's head tipped right back. How to pick this tiny creature up? By the fingers? Surely they'd break off. Little rice kernels.
Squeeze his belly? He'd puke.

Under his armpits, Sara.

Right. I grabbed it under the arms, a slithering ball of Silly
Putty between my palms.

His head. Hold his head.

Got it.

The thing started to scream. A shaky, high-pitched ghoulish
noise I'd never heard before. I bounced at the knee with baby in
my hands, a rotten tomato with extremities. He reminded me
of the barbecued pigs that hung in Chinatown shop windows. I
thought of placing my large palm across his face, I thought of
shoving him between the couch cushions, I thought of letting go.

I handed the baby back to Jenny, extra carefully, and ran
home.

Nik was on the sofa, sweater-vested and slacked, stroking Asslan.
I curled up at Nik's feet and lay my head on his lap next to
Asslan's. Asslan swatted at me.

I almost killed Jenny's baby.

Babies are easy to kill.

No, I whispered. I thought about ways to kill it.

I think about ways to kill you sometimes.

Pillow in the face?

Cyanide in the Engevita yeast.

You always know the right thing to say.

Hey Sara.

Did you know how to take care of a baby right away?

Still don't.

How did we survive?

It's a blur. Honestly.

How do people do this right?

They don't.

~~THE EIGHTH MONTH~~ *Baby Advice. Take It or Shake It*

My last hurrah took place in Nik's mom's living room. A herd of eager-faced, silk-bloused realtors surrounded me. A hair-sprayed pastel colour wheel. To my right, Jenny and babe. To my left, Jackie the Viking doula. The realtors presented me with offerings of onesies and Baby Einstein DVDs. They all feigned interest in Jenny's baby by making overdramatic smiley faces from afar and poking his belly as they approached. To ignore him on this day would be sacrilegious.

We ate toothpick-speared melons and cherry tomatoes and drank chamomile tea and the ladies gave advice to Jenny and me. Don't forget your husband's needs. Stop nursing after four months. Let baby cry it out. Sleep baby on its front. Don't use cloth. Attend to baby's every cry. Sleep baby on its back. Nurse until baby's two, at least.

When the ladies tired of gasping at Jenny's baby, Nik's mom brought out the Prosecco and Celine Dion. All the realtors performed a high-elbowed dance around Jenny, Jackie and me. Collingwood's top seller stumbled on an unruly loop of carpet and came within an inch of heeling Jenny's baby in the navel. Jenny was busy filling her cheeks with cantaloupe so I picked the little fella up by the pits, my fingertips against the back of his head for support. His apricot bum rested on my belly. This time, he didn't look so porkish. He was open-eyed and silent. And when I flapped my lips at him I swear he smiled. Nik's mom spotted me under the frame of her pit-stained sleeve and gave me a thumbs-up.

Sara?
I'm getting close. Eight months.
Home stretch.
I might stop calling you.
Suit yourself.
That's it?
You owe me nothing, I owe you nothing.
You're my mother.
And?
Nothing.

~~THE NINTH MONTH~~ *Bring It*

The afternoon we became four, Nik, Asslan and I sunned our-selves through our bedroom window. We pretended our bed was a Hawaiian island and our floor was the sea. Nik drew a Sharpie grid on my belly and we played checkers with blanched and unblanched almonds. And then, there was an almalanche.

Hey, Nik said. Poor sport.

I didn't do it.

Juniper?

My body imploded in fits and starts, consuming the baby before ejecting it. Nik called Jackie and grabbed me a pair of clean underwear. We ran outside holding hands and headed west. After two blocks I stopped and asked Nik where we were going.

I don't know, he said, I'm following you.

I'm following you.

Nik looked at his watch. The 106 should be here soon.

Can you take the bus when you're in labour?

Nik laid his jacket down on the bus stop bench so as to protect my birth canal from potential pollutants and we sat and waited. Whenever a bus approached, Nik squeezed my hand, then released when it wasn't ours. An old lady navigated a shopping trolley full of baguettes and Boost over shovelled-snow piles and around our bench. Nik and I lifted our feet to accommodate her but she didn't notice. Was there no unavoidable aura surrounding us on that day, compelling her to stare? I looked up at our reflection in the windows of passing vehicles. Those two couldn't possibly be me and Nik. Those two looked like they were about to do something.

At the hospital I felt like I was having a bad menstrual cramp every few minutes. Women's screams echoed through the halls of the delivery ward. It sounded like I was trapped in either a porn film or ladies' night in hell. Then the period cramps felt like a tsunami of periods, not a shedding of my uterine lining but of my entire uterus, my organs, myself. I crawled onto the hospital bed and embodied Cat Bjelland from that night a year ago when Nik and I watched her have kittens. Rubbed up against the Boo Radley house on her front paws, ass high, scratching at the grass with her hind legs. She yowled like a human baby, her eyes wide and fixed with each stoic convulsion. Every time a slick oval of goo slopped out of her, she curled over to lick it clean. I wondered how she knew what to do. And would my baby come out like a slimy sea otter? What if my tongue wasn't strong enough?

When my yowling began, Nik let me crush his fingers into my palm. He wiped the hair from my face with his free hand and whispered, Good kitty, to me while Jackie pounded oil that smelled too much like basic-bitch mango onto my back. When my little nugget slopped out, a goo-licking was not required but I did lick her—once on the nose—so I'd feel like a real mother.

You didn't stop calling.
I had the baby. I thought you might want to know.
Congratulations.
Ten fingers, ten toes. A girl.
What's her name?
Juniper, maybe. Holly? A bush of some sort.
You'll be great, Sara.
Thanks.
Not like me.
Forget it.

~~POSTPARTUM~~ *You're in This for Life*

I spent the first few weeks naked in bed with Juniper cuddled to my chest like a warm lump of biscuit dough. While she nursed I crooked my nose to her scalp and breathed in sweet baby. When Nik came home, he bookended Juni and conjoined noses with me.

What will this smell like when she's sixteen?

Grease and pomade.

When she's seven?

Lollipops.

When she's one?

Like this, but slightly corrupted.

I stared at Juni's head for a minute, pictured it billowed in teenaged form. I bumped my finger along her downy chub and stopped at her ankle, circled it like a string on a balloon.

Big Spoon

I met Rocco the day I fell up the stairs and spilled Mom's groceries onto the third floor of her building. A shift's worth of wages at the coffee shop bruised and strewn all over a dusty linoleum floor. I yelled, Fuck me. Rocco poked his head out of 3A and said, If I help will you give me a banana? He was beautiful. Tall, olive-skinned, thick black hair, eyes capable of swallowing the world. All I could do was nod.

He didn't actually help me. He grabbed a banana and ate it while I shoved heads of iceberg lettuce, processed cheese, wieners and all their unsavoury peers into cloth bags.

You live here?

No, my mom does. 4A.

Sketchy Sue?

Her name's not Sue.

I don't say that to her face.

It's Gwen.

Sketchy Sue's a better fit.

Shut up, I said, and smacked his shoulder like a giddy pre-teen addressing a boy who'd yanked her training bra strap.

Pleased to meet you, Sketch Junior. I'm Rocco.

Meg.

You loopy like Sue?

Don't call her loopy.

She can't shop for herself?

She doesn't leave her apartment much.

Lifeline? Rocco shot me with his finger gun.

I guess. I have a sister, but she's... I fluttered my hand above my head.

A butterfly?

No. Sort of. She took off when I was fourteen. Winnipeg, I think. To find our father.

Harsh.

I nodded. Rocco periscoped his arm and threw his banana peel to an imaginary garbage. It smacked against the wall across from us and landed at our feet. He grabbed my hand and said, Girl, why they keep movin' the trash can?

We sat a while, in silence, toeing a can of Chunky soup back and forth until it rolled too far away for either of us to reach.

If I pick that up will you give me a beej? he said.

It would take more effort to blow you than to pick up that can.

Fine, he said. Sit on my bed with me.

I have a boyfriend.

Doesn't seem like it, he said.

He got up and walked into his apartment. I followed, even though Mom had texted me for Kraft Dinner and Corona an hour earlier, and a few blocks away Alex teetered off the edge of one of my kitchen chairs and flipped through my copy of *BUST* in order to keep abreast (no pun intended) of the issues pertaining to me in the least imposing manner possible. I followed

Rocco because he was right. I did have a boyfriend but it didn't seem like it. Alex and I had been together nine months but we hadn't boned since our sixth date: tacos and a one-sided conversation about Baudrillard's abolition of death concept followed by a one-sided missionary-style orgasm.

When I suggested the meal between the sheets hadn't satisfied and would he mind another taco, he rolled over and spent the rest of the night sobbing over his inadequacies. After that, he only wanted to cuddle. That word made me shudder. An hour and a half of spooning and guessing letters traced on the other's back with no promise of an orgasm. Once, I masturbated while he drew I LOVE YOU with his pinky between my shoulder blades and he told me I had sullied the intimacy of the act. After that, I had to conceal it—lie on my stomach, tell him I splayed my wrist under my crotch in order to stretch out my carpal tunnel, fake sneezing when I convulsed. I ached for a cock in me.

Rocco's apartment was one room. A lone toilet sat in the back right corner at an angle as though a giant had flicked it while playing dolls. A counter jutted from behind the apartment door, holding a sink, a crevassed bar of soap and a crumbly trail of ketchup chips. Black outlines of big-eyed women with small pointed breasts and crooked T. Rex arms were painted onto his walls.

You're an artist?

Rocco sat on his bed, legs crossed, eyes closed. Sit with me, he said.

My roommate's an artist. Clair Holmes? You know her?

Is she hot?

In a gaunt, big-nosed, Velcro-haired sort of way.

Then probably not. Come here. Rocco held his arm out to me.

I took his hand and climbed into his lap, face to face. A bulb of his shoulder blade in each palm, I breathed. He fisted a clump of hair at my crown, clenched and released with each inhale and exhale. We didn't speak. He didn't ask questions. Where have you been? What are you doing? What aren't you doing? Nothing.

Rocco's long lean fingers squeezed my throat. I grabbed his wrist, my jaw dropped. His other palm fell to the small of my back, pressed me closer, winded me, my heels to his hip bones. His fingers, my fingers between my heels. He drove down on my throat, to the bed. He halved me head to tail with his fingertip. Exclamation mark.

You like that, darlin'? he said, his wrist twitching. You like it rough?

I nodded and pulled at his T-shirt, pulled him close, his mouth to my ear.

What's your boyfriend like? he said.

He's hipper than all the plaid in a logging camp.

Hipper than a flat white?

Hipper than the barista who made it.

Hipper than the stylist who waxed his moustache?

Stop.

What?

Stop talking about him.

Rocco nosed my neck. What are you doing here, darlin'? I could be a serial killer.

Maybe that's why I'm here.

I will paint you, he said, in a way that meant not right now or tomorrow or the next day, but in an intended future that only existed in the minds of people like me.

I pushed him off and said, I should go before you kill me.

I gathered Mom's groceries and Rocco slid his torso up against the wall. He gazed at one of his two-dimensional girls with his arm overhead, as though posed for a fragrance ad. Irreverence, for men.

Will I see you again?

Probably, he said. Small building.

Okay, well. Okay. I stood at the foot of his bed and waited for things to shift slightly in my direction. I wanted a parting ceremony. An outstretched arm. A gesture of cling. After a full breath's pause, I said, Later, but it came out as a high-pitched question, not the gravel-voiced indifference I was going for.

Mom was splayed in front of the TV upstairs in 4A. A lime-wedge sailboat drifted in a drying puddle of Corona on the carpet below. She was edging toward sobriety by switching her poison every few weeks, each drink of choice weaker than its predecessor. Vodka to wine to beer. She'd been stuck on Corona for months now. I shelved her groceries, poured a bowl of dry Cheerios and placed it in the nook behind her knees. On my way out I turned off the TV but this woke her.

She wriggled, rattling the Cheerios, and said, Why did it get so lonely in here?

Do you want the TV back on, Mom?

Change it to CBC. *Mr. Bean.*

There's a bowl of Cheerios behind you.

Good girl.

Mom ate a couple Cheerios and grabbed an empty Corona bottle from the floor, shook it side to side. I pretended I didn't see. Meg? she said, shaking her bottle.

I brought some food, Mom.

I'm running out.

Of what?

She held the bottle above her head.

What are you running out of, Mom?

Pasta, I guess.

I brought Kraft Dinner.

Make me some?

Alex is waiting.

Cup of tea?

Sure.

Mom rose from the couch and I could tell from the plaid imprints on her thighs she'd been there all night. I met a guy last night, she said.

Oh yeah?

Christian. His name, I think. Or maybe he was.

Nice to you?

Good dancer.

I'm glad you got out.

I get out. Ellen dragged me.

I met someone too.

What about Alex?

3A. You know him?

The Paintbrush Cowboy.

Rocco?

I don't like the way he looks at me. Penetrating.

I think I'm tired of Alex.

Kid is way too needy.

You've never met him.

You're more sloped, past few months.

Didn't realize you watched me.

Mom turned off the kettle and slopped boiling water into two mugs. Want milk, Meggie?

I always want milk.

He spent the night.

Christian?

Passed out on the floor, but still.

Rocco asked me onto his bed. There was no reason not to. Is that cheating?

What is cheating? What are rules?

I'd be pissed if Alex did that.

Maybe he has.

Did my father cheat?

Mom stared at me, eyes glazed, cheeks drooped, lips sphinctered, then looked into her cup of tea. I can't live on tea alone, Meg.

I filled your cupboards.

Christian might come over tonight. He might want a drink.

Then he might need to bring it.

Just like your sister. Your father.

Thanks for the cuppa.

Mom flicked her wrist and sloshed tea onto the wall beside her. She stared at it a few seconds. Damn it, Meg, she said.

I wet a cloth that had been curled around her kitchen tap, starched stiff with neglect, and handed it to her. She didn't thank me. She silently scrubbed, her head bobbing with the effort.

I rested a hand on her shoulder. Take it easy, Mom. Don't spend your whole cheque on him.

I returned home to Alex, his torso draped over my kitchen table next to two cups of Bengal Spice. It looked as though the tiger on the tea box stalked him. I told him to watch out.

What?

The tiger. I held my hands, claw-shaped, above his forehead.

How's your mom?

Still drinking Corona.

I'm sorry to hear that.

That was all Alex ever said. I failed an exam. I'm sorry to hear that. I've run out of toilet paper. I'm sorry to hear that. The only soup they're serving is carrot ginger. I'm sorry to hear that.

What does that even mean?

Pardon?

I'm sorry to hear that. It's all about you.

You are so selfish, Meg.

My roommate Clair walked in and sat next to Alex and in front of the second cup of Bengal Spice.

Oh, I said. I thought that was for me.

Sorry, Clair said. You took so long, Alexander made me some. Clair cradled the cup with her boney, claw-fingered hand and I swore she slid it an inch closer to Alex's.

Didn't know I was operating on a schedule.

Alex removed his glasses, looked at me with his myopic clove eyes and said, *I'll be right back* doesn't usually mean *I'm going to take three hours to deliver groceries to my mother.*

We had a conversation. A cup of tea.

Great progress, Meg. Clair smiled at me with that stupid sweet smile that made me regret telling her anything about anything.

Clair and I went to high school together but were never friends. She was one of those cliqueless girls who did yearbook and ran on the cross-country team. I wore fishnets and shorty shorts and listened to screamy girl bands. She dressed in high-waisted pleated slacks and turtlenecks and was nice to everyone. You couldn't dislike her, no matter how much you wanted to. She ended up in some of my art history courses in university. When she told me she was looking for a place to live I thought, how imposing could a girl who plays Pictionary and dresses like a celibate archivist be? It started with my tea cupboard and her Bengal Spice and fruit zingers and whatnot. Then she started to call my boyfriend Alexander. Wore her most body-hugging turtlenecks when he came over. Listened sympathetically when he whined about his fear of death.

Progress? I said. I guess, but she threw tea at me.

Alex laughed, put his glasses back on and, in so doing, elbowed Clair in the nose. For that unconscious loyalty, I loved him.

Her actions say more about her than you, Clair said. Clair was always reading some floral-patterned, cursive-fonted self-help book. She spouted a new set of rules for living with the completion of each volume.

Sorry for laughing. Alex sipped his tea, and in so doing, brushed his hand against Clair's over-neighbourly hand. For this conscious betrayal, I hated him.

I also hung out for a bit with my mom's neighbour. This artist, Rocco. You know him, Clair?

Clair nodded. By reputation only.

He's good?

He's a playboy.

That makes sense.

Alex jerked his head toward me. Excuse me?

He asked me to blow him.

Alex and Clair each choked a little.

Did you? Alex said.

Clair rose from the table in one impressive motion. No hands. I guess when you weigh eighty pounds you're limber like that. She was bird-like, but not in a swallowish, skittery way. Clair was more hawk. Hooked nose, deep-set eyes. Circling disposition. I'll go to my room, she said.

Did you? Alex repeated.

Do you have to ask?

Alex removed his glasses. Does that mean yes or no?

You're fucking Clair, aren't you?

Alex smashed his glasses into the kitchen table. One of the arms broke off and slid across the floor until it came to a sludgey halt in a rancid, buttery wad of popcorn kernels collected near the fridge. He shook his head, looked up at me, separated his lips, inhaled in preparation for a proclamation, then changed his mind.

Why are you here?

To be with you, he said.

But I wasn't home.

I was waiting for you.

With Clair. All you need is a warm body. Open ears, open arms. It's not about me.

Do you know what I did while you were out? I lay on your bed with my head on your pillow because it smelled like you.

But that's the problem. I said this to my knees, folded against the edge of the kitchen table. You only love the ghost of me.

I wish you and your mother the best. Alex stood up and brushed his hands against one another, even though they were perfectly crumb-free. Typical dramatic Alex gesture.

Are you coming back?

Not for you, he said. And Alex grabbed his glasses and walked out without a glance at their phantom limb.

I felt like I'd left a meaningless conversation. Sad—not to be alone, but for the loss of what I'd hoped would feel less lonely. I trudged to my room and looked at my pillow, slathered in the pungent, earthy smell of Alex's hair I alternately loved and hated. I ripped off my pillowcase. Clair knocked on my door ten minutes later, head tilted to the right and full of advice. She clawed at my shoulder in an attempt at compassion.

If it was meant to be, you'll come back together.

I don't think I ever liked him.

He cares for you a lot.

Like he cares for that drooling guy in the wheelchair on Government.

You can't fault him his big heart.

He has a big head. No heart.

I invited him to this art party Friday. I didn't know you two would, you know.

Art party?

I'm showing one of my nudes.

Clair was too square to deserve the title *artist*. She'd had one show of horrifyingly modest nudes in some divey, doilie-infested tea house in James Bay and she called herself an artist. I could only imagine what sort of hairless, scolio-backed creature, hunched into itself as though shipwrecked, would be on display.

Who else is showing?

Some recent fine arts grads.

I looked out the window, nonchalant. If Clair understood me at all, she would've told me whether Rocco would be there. He didn't seem like a recent graduate. Creased lips, face heavy with silvering stubble. His were not the eyes that hoped to make a living as an artist. He ran on luck, laziness, entitlement. Gifts of bananas and sexual favours. Potassium, fructose and ejaculate protein. Maybe he was a gigolo. Maybe he had an upper-middle-class benefactor.

Maybe I'll go too.

—

Friday night I played the sisterhood card, convinced Clair to unin-vite Alex and take me to the party. She led me to an old house in Fernwood, big and haphazard as though it was built one room at a time. Inside, the air was thin like everyone had inhaled more than their share and then blew it out hot and self-aggrandizing. Clair showed me her friends' work: paint-by-numbers puppies, geometric shapes in primary colours, collages of recycling-bin items glue-gunned to cupboard doors found on the side of the road. Outside the laundry room hung Clair's nude. A disembod-ied red cardigan, unravelled enough to reveal one boob. One small, peach-coloured nipple.

I peeked into the laundry room and saw Rocco fingering some curvy girl against the washing machine. She had one pil-lowy leg draped over his shoulder and out the door. I could've tickled her toes. Rocco bent, head pressed into her armpit, legs in volleyball ready position, spasmodic twitching arm. I heard him say, You like that, Lizzie? The other woman was always a deriv-ative of Elizabeth. Lizzie, Liz, Beth. Sometimes Zsa Zsa. *Darlin'* was more intimate. Maybe he'd forgotten my name.

In the kitchen, a trio of neo-hippies discussed sprouts and almond mylk. To their left, on the living room floor atop a pile of meditation cushions, sat Alex, legs swizzled long and awkward in front, an unravelled lotus.

Meg. You're here. Alex's eyes were bloodshot and puffy. I would've liked to believe he'd been crying over me for the past two days but I knew he was allergic to his contacts.

I thought you were uninvited. I turned to Clair.

Hand to mouth, Clair mumbled, I forgot.

Did you enjoy Clair's nude?

Very much, Alex said.

Really, Alexander? While I was painting you said it wasn't provocative enough.

It's plenty provocative, I said. What's with *Alexander*, Clair?

It's my name. Alex stood up in front of me, hands on hips, assertive.

I call you Alex.

What are you, three?

What are you, a Russian tsar?

You don't need to say Russian. It's redundant.

I guess Clair would know that.

We've never discussed pre-revolutionary Russia. Alex hooked his thumbs into his belt loops and hiked his pants up a bit. He was so bland, so even-toned, he had to punctuate his statements with movement. Hand brushes, spectacle slides, foot stomps, door slams.

I stared at Alex. From behind I could hear the washer rock like it was imbalanced with a thick, nymphomaniacal rug. I wanted to stop everything. I wanted Alex to come home with me and lie in my bed and talk about *World of Warcraft* so I could revel in the safety of his geekiness. Or tell me he wanted us to be cryogenically frozen until they found a cure for death and I'd hold him and run my lips along his stubble like I used to do with my Velcro sneakers as a kid. I'd write STAY on his back but by the time he guessed it the sentiment would be gone. Then he'd gingerly tuck me in and stick to his side until morning. I'd wish he'd steal the covers and drool into my hair instead.

I felt a hand on my waist. Rocco. Sketch Junior, he said.

It's Meg.

What're you doing later? he spat into my ear.

I saw you fingering a Rubens.

Was it porn worthy?

I shook my head. Like you were assembling furniture.

Alex hiked his pants again, this time to moose-knuckle heights. I don't believe we've met, he said. I'm Meg's boyfriend.

Hey, Meg's boyfriend. I'm Rocco.

I thought we broke up, I said.

I said I wouldn't come back for you. That's not a breakup.

Pretty hard to date someone who only comes for your roommate.

You did the cardigan painting? Rocco said to Clair.

Clair nodded.

Your own tit?

Clair nodded.

Your nipple's really that PG?

Clair looked at Rocco. She bopped her head like a pigeon, most likely sifting through a barrage of self-help catchphrase matches for the situation. I prefer not to discuss the subject of my art, she said, but I thank you for speaking your truth.

Rocco wrapped his hand around my neck and pulled me toward him. Come over next time you visit your mom, eh?

He waved at all of us and walked off, fingers wiggling.

That's the guy? Alex said. How could you want that? He just strangled you.

And then he let go.

Outside the party, the air smelled of wet leaves and rotting apples. Maple leaves piled high enough to house a family of rabbits lined the road. I wanted to be whimsical and fly-by-the-seat-of-my-pants zany, so I flopped down on one and rolled. It was fun. If I was actually whimsical, I wouldn't think it was fun, I would do the fun. I would fun. And I wouldn't wonder why Alex witnessed the painting of Clair's nipple. When? How? Since when does he like *provocative*?

The last time I felt close to Alex, months earlier, we drank tea in bed. The pot warm between my thighs, his middle finger dawdled along the arch of my foot. I told him to stop drinking. If we didn't finish the pot the moment would last forever. He told me he lived beyond the moment, to its eventual demise, when the pot grew cold and his finger tired. I spent so much effort dragging him out of the black hole of his mortality, he never noticed the puddle I treaded.

Mom texted: *fight with guy. no corona. help mom.*

I dug myself deeper into the leaves, covered my face and wondered if I could die there. Would I allow myself the smothering? My phone buzzed again and I came out for air.

Mom texted: *hello?????*

I didn't reply, but I did get up. I did go to the liquor store. I did knock on 3A. No answer.

In 4A, Mom slept in her bed. Beer bottles lay scattered across the living room like bowling pins. Strike. A list on the fridge: *Pasta / Corona / Meg.* Mom's life in three lines.

She looked like a toddler who'd collapsed after a tantrum. Saggy underwear puckered up her butt cheeks like a withered balloon, bed sheets twisted around her wrists. I lay down behind her, rested a hand on her shoulder.

Christian man?

It's Meg.

Mom lifted a hand to my hand on her shoulder. He came for you, she said.

Alex?

Paintbrush Cowboy. Left an address where he'll be tonight.

I'll see him some other time. I lowered my arm to Mom's waist, slim but squishy, like a water balloon gaping toward the mattress. Okay if I sleep here?

Bad dream?

Monster under my bed.

Mom laughed, and her breathing slowed. I matched my breath to hers and we slept. I didn't even think about waking up.

Angling

It's been three years since you held the title *student*. Since you left the ivory-towered microcosm in which you held importance, promise, direction. You have a degree in art history, an apartment, a job as an overqualified barista—trapped in purgatory between teenager and grown-up. You have no means to justify your existence on this planet aside from caffeinating hipsters, hacks and high school–hooky players. Until convocation, all was preordained. Now you don't know what, how, when the secrets of life will be divulged. You spend your time making plans you'll never carry out. All potential next steps come with a list of prerequisites you don't have the energy or commitment to fulfill.

This cute guy frequents the café where you work. Every time with the LSAT book. Skinny jeans precisely rolled. Well-kept moustache. Canvas loafers. Hip lawyer. Lawyer without a cause. He wants to talk to you. He orders fancy espresso drinks. Inquires, What's a flat white? How does it compare to a latte? They're continents apart, you say. He laughs. Too hard. The joke was lame and you both know it. It's embarrassing, his laughter. He tips in bills. I hope you're not expecting special treatment, you say. He opens his mouth but only hiccups with a constipated wit. He retreats to his table. You don't care. He's a distraction. A month ago, Rocco left for Montreal. *I can't be an artist in Victoria. You can be an artist anywhere. I can't be an artist with you.* On, off, on again, off again, on again, off. Time to move on.

The next day, the cute guy comes in later than usual. Last night's clothes, steeped in some undergrad's drugstore perfume. The morning after is one size too big on him. He's bold, introduces himself. When you hear him say *Tom*, you relax. Tom is the name of a bus driver, a best friend's father, a husband watching his cholesterol. You buy Tom clothes at Value Village. Dress him as Rocco. Ratty T-shirts two sizes too small with funny sayings like *Superfreak, Hugs Not Drugs, Unicorns Are Horny.* There's a Snugli in one of the bins, tossed there by accident. I think we need this, he says. You've become a *we.* A hand holder. A crook-of-the-arm rester. A better half. Domesticated, constructed.

At your apartment—his apartment—Tom wears the Snugli, inserts your teddy bear as baby. Let's go for a walk, he says. You take turns with the baby in the Snugli. Hold hands. Make plans. Have visions. Hallucinations. Kids, career, patio furniture. Family car, stray cat, PAC meetings, sick days, Christmas stockings.

He kneels and grabs your hand at the corner of Rockland and Moss, umbrellaed by elderly pine. Meg, he says. You like the way he says your name. The way other people say *God.* Oh, Meg. Oh, God. You need to move on. Need to be a grown-up. Need to protect yourself from cellulite, elephant skin, spider veins, nursing homes, becoming your mother, dying alone. You say, Yes. You kiss Tom. Think about his tongue. Its sluggishness. Think about breathing through your mouth again. Think about not thinking.

—

We're getting married, you say. You should meet my mother. Tom is ecstatic. He can check it off his list. Your mother is hesitant, but she's cleaned her apartment. Tidied. The black footprints on the carpet remain, the mildewed bathroom towels, the nests of fallen hairs. She turns off the TV. Serves corn chips and guacamole. Impressive.

Corona, anyone? She laughs and waves her bottle.

No, Mom.

Sure, Tom says. Why not?

Oh, Meg, she says, like *Oh, fuck*. Live a little.

You should see her when she's not drunk, you say to no one.

Mom and Tom predict your future. Spring wedding, lilies and cherry blossoms, small ceremony, registry at the Bay, unimmaculate conception, one and a half kids, mom groups, law degree, house in Hillside, sex on Tuesdays and Saturdays, soccer, gymnastics, art class, trips to Disneyland, cabin on a Gulf island, summer camp, book clubs, potlucks, philanthropy, post-secondary education, empty nest, retirement, Hawaii, cruises, prescription drugs, cancer, nurses, home care, last will and testament, death, cremation, funeral, dedicated park bench.

It's easier than you imagined to create a boy. Should anyone be allowed to do this? You and Tom collect things. Small things. Tiny socks, mittens, chew toys. Think of names. Tom Jr., Ezekiel, Jebediah, Nimrod. Like it's a doll. A joke. A game. Tom worships your belly. Rubs it like it's enchanted. He doesn't look you in the eye, only in the navel. The window to your purpose, your third eye. Tom decides on Sebastian. I was bitten by a dog named Sebastian, you say. Sebastian, he says.

You quit the café, stay at home, mother. Stroller walks, tummy time, nap time. You have a perpetual sense of lack. You've missed an important game, book, vitamin essential to Sebastian's development, to your bond. You fall in love with him in his sleep. Wonder if it is love or narcissism. Soft peach cheeks, searching lips. Does he dream of milk? If only your needs were pared down to one. When his lids separate you curse your lost time, space, sleep.

Tom goes to school. Returns, tosses the baby, pat-a-cakes, retreats. You give. Give life, give milk, give baths, give head. Tom says, You're still sexy, as though it's understood you're not. Your navel has recessed an inch into the vat of skin you used to call your midriff. You can't remember what you looked like before.

You do remember Rocco. The way he squeezed you under the ribs and said, *I love your tiny little body. I love that it's mine.* The way you felt naked for him alone. Trusted him wholly with your flesh. In a recurring dream, you find Rocco in the hall outside your apartment. Tight-jeaned and waifish, his dark curls woven into the neighbour's door. You touch his arm, he turns and tells you, *It's too big here.* Awake, Tom's arm constricts across your ribs. You label it love but it feels like obligation. You thought life would be easier with a man. Messy, hungry, horny man. You didn't know. You didn't have a father.

Shadowed by husband and child, by their expectations, you feel absolutely alone. You miss high school, where labels could be sloughed off like garments when they pinched. Prep, Goth, Emo. These—Wife, Mother—stick. But the wardrobe is not prescribed, your mouth fumbles over the new language. Your lips struggle to stretch around the word *compromise*. Tom floats in and out of the house to study, exercise, unwind. He expresses all of his needs as essential. Master of spin-doctory. Lawyer without a cause. You have become foundation, a load-bearing stud. To leave the house now requires an argument, a deposition, a get-out-of-jail-free card.

Virtual escape, however, is sanctioned. Easily concealed. You seek Wi-Fied connection. High school acquaintances, ex-boyfriends. You find old friends on Facebook, peruse their photos, forget about them all over again. Trawl dating sites as *Megalomaniac* for Rocco look-alikes. Applicants must be over six feet tall and under one hundred thirty pounds, have fingernails wedged with acrylics and smell of rancid butter and marinara sauce. Must look at you—into you—with a cocktail of indifference and animal lust. Your suitors could be Rocco's grease-stained, chopper-riding uncle; his hairy-backed, sweaty-foreheaded barber; his meth-addicted, adolescent-complected half brother. With your right pointer, you peck out declines to their offers of cocks to suck and bulldogs to befriend, Sebastian with his leaking mouth and bashing palms crooked into your left elbow. What you want is to not be needed. To be left. Rocco. Your father.

Your father's not on the internet. Not even an employee listing, a letter to the editor, a running race result. There are not enough Damian Costellos in the world, but there is Kneel Young on Plenty of Fish. His photo wrings the air from your lungs. Like you've seen it in a dream. He shares your pointed chin and almond eyes. He fits the profile. Claims to be thirty-five, which is what any fifty-year-old cruising twenty-five-year-olds would do. From Victoria, currently in Vancouver. Plays guitar. Occupation: living, man. Married once. Two daughters. His honesty surprises you. But chicks love a guy with daughters. The clincher: favourite things include jelly beans. Jellybean. That was his nickname for your sister. Who likes jelly beans? It must be him. You send him a message. Rather, Megalomaniac does. *How old are your daughters? Why do you like jelly beans?*

Kneel Young waits a week to reply. *My daughters are grown. Jelly beans remind me of them.*

You're thirty-five, you write. *You had kids when you were fifteen?*

You're blunt, he replies. *Meet me.*

We're an ocean apart.

I'd cross that ocean for you.

With the help of stardust and BC Ferries?

And pixies and sprites.

You don't tell Tom about your father. That would make it less real. Less your own. Tom would want a reason. Boredom, curiosity, loneliness. Talking Oozi-Boo to a drooling flesh meringue all day. Baby-shit hands, T-shirts wet with rotting milk. Stimulation, conversation. Guidance, imitation. Something outside Tom's realm of influence.

Kneel Young persists. *Meet me, meet me on a train. Meet me, meet me in a plane. Meet me, meet me with a goat. Meet me, meet me on a boat.* You persist. *What are your daughters' names? What's your name? Tell me about your ex-wife.* He evades. *Meet me at Beacon Hill Farm. I'll be with the goats. Meet me on Government. I'll be sucking gelato off a beaver tail. Meet me in Fernwood square. I'll be slacking.*

Tom is suspicious. You're spending a lot of time on the computer.

Research, you say.

For what?

Life. Grad school, maybe. Gender studies?

But you're a mother.

A mother can't have a life?

That's not what I meant.

Then why did you say that?

Say what?

You know what.

He smacks his two hands against the wall. The way you wish he'd touch you. I can't talk to you, he says.

Then don't.

You both stay. Statues. Ice sculptures. How hard would it be to melt? Wrap your hands around him, grab his crotch. Say, *Is that a gun in your pocket?* He would laugh. Turn to you. You could fall into him. Rub your cheek against his stubble. His furry warmth. His kiss, like home. Safe and comfortable. Sometimes annoyingly so. But then Sebastian would cry. Tom would say, *The baby.* What those two words have come to mean: Take care of that, make it stop. You leave him, hands against the wall. To your bed, your laptop. *Meet me, meet me with the goats.*

Your mother holds Sebastian by the armpits, her chin pulled in as though only the webbing between her thumbs and index fingers could handle his toxicity. She asks if he eats olives because that's all she has in the refrigerator and you leave him with her anyway. You advise her to stick with Cheerios and then cross a threshold free of baby for the first time in eight months.

Kneel Young sits on a rock in Beacon Hill Farm among the goats but he has no takers. The goats prefer children. Small, dirty, no sense of self. Animal. He looks like a man you'd catch muttering to himself on the bus. Shoulder-length blond-grey drips of hair emanate from a peninsula atop his crown. He's squeezed into a pink golf shirt with a white deodorant ring around each armpit. You could leave. He'd never know. You could end this now. He's come all this way. You touch his shoulder. He looks up, uncertain, vulnerable. The father you knew in your imagination as cool, indifferent.

You showed, he says.

I did.

Rockin'.

Should we go somewhere?

I thought you'd never ask.

He's your father. He puts his arm around your waist. That's acceptable. Father–daughter. Will you tell me your name now?

What's yours?

My name's Phoebe.

I'm Gerald.

Actually, Meg.

Okay, Damian.

Damian?

Friends call me Dams.

You walk with Damian, your father, on Dallas Road, along a cliff above the ocean. He holds your hand. That's acceptable. Father–daughter. You block out the disparity between the nature of his desire and yours. Your father holds your hand. Touches you. Here. Now.

So is your wife dead? you say.

Do I look that old?

Why are you single?

Why are you?

I asked first.

She's not dead.

You sure?

Guess not. I took off on her a long time ago.

How did it fall apart? you say.

I had a punk band, Dorothy's Rainbow. I always hated the name, he says. We were going to be ska. One night my second bassist brought this girl to our show. She told me our set sucked. We did suck. Three-chord wonders. Two-and-a-half-chord wonders. I got her pregnant. We married. Had another kid. A family. I tried to make it work but it wasn't me.

What?

Responsibility, I guess.

You left your family for Dorothy's Rainbow?

No, he says. He looks out to the tankers, the mist, Washington. Left them too.

Do you think about them?

The band?

Your daughters.

I try not to.

Maybe they think about you.

Doubt it.

You're their father.

I was barely there.

Have they tried to find you?

Why would they?

They have your blood.

What is blood?

Life, everything.

Why are we talking about my daughters? He grabs your waist with both hands. You're beautiful.

You shove your fists into his chest. What was it like, though, when you were with them?

He holds your hands. Runs his thumbs up and over the bulbs of your wrists. Circles your knuckles. It was hell on earth. Beautiful chaos. The love of a child.

You nod. He squeezes your hands.

Why did you leave?

Freedom, he says.

Isn't that selfish?

What good is a father who can't breathe?

What if their mom couldn't breathe either?

She was fine. She told me not to come back.

She didn't mean that.

He looks at you, suspicious. The knowing in your voice. He moves his fingers up your forearms. Come here. You're beautiful.

You already said that.

One kiss.

Tell me something good about yourself.

I vote NDP.

I vote Green.

You win.

I have to go.

Don't leave, Meg.

You're one to talk, you say. Your father drops your arms.

You've crossed a line. You hate him. You love him. You want him to take you away. You want to be him. You miss Sebastian. The love of a child. You want to jump off this cliff and float away.

Did it make you happy? you say. He shoves his hands into his pockets and swings his hips toward you, away from you. He smells fungal. His hair scutters around his cheeks in the wind like paint peeling from an old beach house.

I'm not happy, he says, but I'm myself.

At home, you attempt to be happy. To savour each moment. Now. Now. And now. But what to savour? Cry. Cry. Whine. Laugh. Cry. From what reserves does one entertain a child? With what energy does one lift lips? You operate in negatives. Not yelling. Not letting go. Not walking away.

Tom notices you're depressed. Says he wants you to be happy. Not a show of care, a request. I want to be happy too, you say.

Well, aren't you?

You stare past him at a splotch of oatmeal on the kitchen wall, compile a mental list of his attractive qualities. Why did you agree to this? Safety. You are safe—from bear attacks, destitution, sexually transmitted infections. From passion, care, gut-wrenching love.

Aren't you? he repeats.

You nod. Be happy. Close your eyes and unleash his pants. Kneel at his feet. Take one thigh in each palm and his cock in your mouth. Don't look at his face, the awe. Try to take pleasure in his. Open your thighs against the leg of his chair. Feel as sexy as he says you are. Take him down your throat. Rise and fall against the leg. Be sexy. Be passion, be care, be gut-wrenching love. Try not to gag.

Kneel Young sends you a message: *Was it something I said?* You could do so much with this. An admission. He left you once, he could leave again.

You said I was beautiful, you reply.

You are beautiful.

I'm not crazy for beautiful.
Too reverent?
Too run of the mill. Try gorgeous, adorable, sublime.
Is it my age?
Not your age, your station.
Is it because I wanted a kiss?
Not the kiss, its genus.
Can we meet again?
Somewhere public, somewhere safe.
Like a shopping mall?
Like a busy road.

Your father meets you on a bench at Cook and Pandora beside the spare-change collector who looks like a young Harrison Ford. Your father brings jelly beans. You bring Sebastian in the Snugli.

You have a growth, he says.

I have a son.

I have daughters.

I know.

You place flavour combinations into his palm. Popcorn-root beer-licorice. Strawberry-vomit-cream soda. He puts his combinations into your mouth. Coconut-raspberry-chocolate pudding. His finger inside your lip. Your wet flesh. You tighten your lips. Jerk your head away.

Your father thumbs toward Young Harrison.

He's too clean to be homeless.

He'd get a quarter if you could smell him?

At least fifty cents.

Generous.

I told you I vote NDP.

I vote Communist.

You said Green.

Good memory.

I don't recall any mention of this. He flicks the Snugli. Is there a husband to go with it?

Him.

Is there? He rests his toes on the ground, bounces his knees.

Would that be a problem?

Maybe.

Then, maybe.

Maybe what?

Maybe I have a husband.

You do or you don't.

In body, not spirit.

One of those.

You have a wife.

Do not.

You're not divorced.

How do you know?

You said so.

I did not.

Good memory.

How did you know that?

You smile. Coy. Stalker, not daughter.

Sebastian whips his head back, pecks at your chest. Arms flapping. Pigeon baby. *Maa ma. Maa ma.* He's fussing, I should go.

Your father pats Sebastian's bum. Shh, shh, there's a good boy. Like a grandpa. Like a pervert. He persists. How did you know I'm not divorced?

You evade. He needs to eat. You stand up. Bounce Sebastian. *Maa ma. Maa ma.*

How did you know?

Lucky guess.

Bullshit. He drops the jelly beans at your feet. All over the grass. You don't know me, Meg.

He says Meg like shit, not God. You don't know shit. You do know you will never see him again. Any future, proper, non-incestuous attempts at connection will be tainted by this one. You will stand next to this bench in silence while Young Harrison collects the fallen jelly beans and then you will share a curt goodbye, perhaps a tepid hug or handshake and your father will leave you for good, again, like the bad date you are.

You mope. Take Sebastian for walks, to playgroups, mix with the good mothers. Kitchen renos, sex-evasion techniques, helicopter versus free-range parenting debates. Watch them drown in domesticity.

Your mind is a stream of messages. Confessional: remember the love of a child? Desperate: call me beautiful, call me anything. Cheeky: was it something I said? Coy: I don't know you, but I could if you let me. Forget about being his daughter. Keep him near. Cling to the possibility of a whole self. The message you do send? Naïve: *You can't leave me again.* Send it again and again and again. His silence is the closest he'll come to parenting you. It grounds you, deprives you of a desired object. Because he said so.

He does leave you again. Removes himself from Plenty of Fish like you're some sort of lunatic. You could continue to search for him: repeat this game, play for the prize of a disinterested father. But would it matter? He said the love of a child, not the love of a father.

You spend time at your mother's. Sort her mail: personal, political, junk. Scrape the jam from her cupboard doors. Return her books to their shelves. Arrange them alphabetically and by genre. Refill her liquid soap dispensers. Buy her deli meat, Cheez Whiz, Hamburger Helper. Carrots, lettuce, tomatoes. Nothing intimidating.

Good girl, she says.

How did it feel when he left?

Did Tom leave?

No—my father.

It felt like I had nothing and everything in all the wrong ways. I wanted to jump out the window.

Thanks for staying inside.

I was too much inside.

Inside nonetheless.

You return home to the study door shut firm. Tom will emerge after midterms. After finals. After convocation. After articling. After making partner. After retirement. But Sebastian is here. Eating, shitting, babbling, here. The way he looks at you as he suckles your breast. Maa ma. Oh, God.

Chorus

D addy takes Sebastian to swimming lessons on the first no-school day of every week. The cold water shrinks up his tummy and the other kids sprinkler around him but when Sebastian goes underwater he can grab the squishy parts of his teacher's arm. Daddy doesn't watch and clap like the mommies do. He goes to the hot wooden room. After swimming they get dressed on the slippy floor and Daddy has a temper. He says, How many times do I have to tell you? Underwear first. Socks last. Sebastian forgets every time.

On the way home, Daddy buys Sebastian an ice cream. Daddy calls it the way home but they drive far away to a store by the ocean. A lady outside the store with shiny pink legs makes a house around her eyes with her hands and leans into the window. She waves and Daddy waves back. The lady with shiny pink legs walks into the ice cream store and thumps a chair up to their table. Daddy says, Fancy meeting you here. This is Daddy's friend Simone.

Sebastian didn't think mommies and daddies had friends. Daddy's friend Simone calls Daddy Tom, like Mommy does.

She looks like Mommy but she has yellow hair and no squishy parts. Sebastian tries to squeeze her cheek but she laughs the way Mommy did that time in the library bathroom when he asked about the hot sauce in her underwears. When Daddy's friend Simone laughs, Daddy touches her shiny pink leg and Sebastian feels a prickle in his not-no-brain (the part that thinks the thinks he doesn't think).

*   *   *

Simone flips her ice cream spoon upside down before she sticks her tongue to its concave side and slurps. Sex appeal may be her intent but she only arouses disgust in Tom. Six weeks ago, when he elbowed her over an errant Garry oak root and she pulled him down with her—when she opened her mouth to laugh but impressed her front teeth into his shoulder instead—he could've ejaculated instantly at the sight of her tongue in sticky white goo.

That was when it had been five months and thirteen days since Tom and his wife last had sex. Tom doesn't even count that time because it was after the Thompsons' Christmas party when, all evening, Meg brandished a bottomless gin and tonic like the torch of liberty and flirted with an abundantly freckled CBC intern with a whiny eighties name. The moment freckle-face left the party, Meg flopped her body against Tom's as though a bus they were riding had hit a pothole, and said, Let's go. Once outside, she pinned him against the Thompsons' fence and mashed her crotch against his flaccid penis. I know you want me, she said. You've wanted this all night. She spun and lifted her skirt, offered that ass he barely recognized. When he came, grateful, Meg sucked his thumb and threw up over the fence.

If Tom doesn't count that time, it has been eight months. For eight months, when he would touch Meg, she gave him a conciliatory smile and pulled an inch further into herself. She told him she was tired, busy, depressed. She told him he was too insistent. How could she desire him when he constantly pawed at her and pressed his pelvis into her buttocks, thighs, forearm like a dog. He ceased romantic advances. He chose self-respect, dignity. He chose porn. He masturbated like a sixteen-year-old boy. In bed with Meg cocooned in her sheets beside him, in the shower with the door locked as Meg and Sebastian yelled for the toilet from the other side, in the car with the morning paper draped across his lap. Meg would brush their stiffened sheets and bath towels with her fingertips and roll her eyes at him, retreat another inch.

Self-pleasure wasn't enough. Tom yearned for flesh, sweat, breath. He joined a running group. Meg mocked him at first: Only you would need to learn to run. When his beer belly disappeared, she likened him to Kermit the Frog.

You've become one of those body fat–less Muppets who hop around together and make people feel bad about themselves. Soon you'll be all about flat arches and 10 ks. Tom believed she was jealous. She had wanted them to degrade together. She had wanted his boyish cheeks to sink into jowls as hers had.

Tom would sidle up to female runners to hear them pant in his ear, to rub his sweaty elbows against theirs. It was almost sufficient. But one night he bumped Simone—the girl in pink spandex whose sweat smelled of bubble gum—too hard. When she fell and then he fell, she seemed to enjoy the feel of his shoulder against her enamel. She bit into him and raised her eyebrows. He understood it was wrong. He's a lawyer. But he felt so estranged from the man who spoke those vows six years earlier it was as though this took place in another world—one without rules or consequences, one he could dab his toe into for a month or two and come out a better man, a better husband.

On Tuesday and Thursday evenings, Tom and Simone have been cutting out of running group to her apartment above the ice cream parlour on Yates where she lives with a stray, unstable cat. Her apartment is filled with signs of the mundane: a crumb-free tablecloth, embroidered hand towels, shampoo for normal hair. Meg's shampoo is always unpredictable: dry, itchy scalp, flyaway. Simone has a princess bed covered with bonbon cushions and Hello Kitty paraphernalia under a pink taffeta sky. A tower of glossy, air-brushed reading material looms beside her pillow. The first few times, Tom enjoyed this rose-tinted haven. Simplicity. Sex. But he soon yearned for Meg's dark cloud of cynicism, her angry-woman novels. The way she used to twitch and moan and kick and scratch. Simone is one step from a blow-up doll, more dead fish than mermaid. Tom feels like he's fucking the babysitter.

Simone taps at the side of her empty ice cream bowl with her spoon. She smiles at Sebastian and shoots miniscule spurts of anxious laughter through the silence. Tom could ask her to tell Sebastian the story of how she was bitten by a duck as a child. He could ask Sebastian to sing "I'm a Little Teapot" for her. But he prefers the silence, the penance for this attempt at a simple escape.

* * *

Tuesday evening, Simone tumbles over to running group and tugs her laces tight. She can feel Tom in the pack, can hear him breathe, the way he double-exhales, *heh-huuuuh*, but she doesn't look at him. She worries he'll look back at her the way he did last Saturday when she ran into him at the ice cream parlour with his kid. That look you get when you've had one too many Mike's Hard Lemonades and there's no turning back.

When they run by Simone's place, Tom guides her toward her door with a wordless hand to the small of her back. Inside, he dumps his shoes and gear in a heap and pounds the hardwood to her room, her bed, where he folds his legs around his cock and strokes it while she fidgets with her sweat-sticky sports bra. It's a little hot, but mostly pervy.

Get over here, is the first thing he says to her. Let me come inside you.

And he does. When this started, he would claw at her shoulder blades and squeeze her between his Clydesdale thighs like they were on the cover of a romance novel. The rugged, Scottish kind. He used to groan terms of endearment into her neck: vanilla-scented goddess, tight-pussied princess. Now she's his spooge cup. Simone rolls onto her side and spreads her *Entertainment Weekly*.

Oh my God, Ben Affleck and Jennifer Garner went on vacation together.

Who? Tom palms Simone's hip bone.

Forget it, old man.

If I'm such an old man, why am I here?

I liked the way you looked at me.

Liked?

Like you needed me. Like I could save you.

Not anymore?

I don't know how you look at me now.

I still need you.

For more than sex?

Of course.

I feel like a warm body.

You're a hot body.

Simone swats away the fingers approaching her crotch. You look at me like you're bored, that's how.

If I were bored, I wouldn't be here.

You should go home to your wife.

I always go home at nine.

You told her we go for three-hour runs?

I need time away.

Your son's cute.

He is.

Is your wife?

Of course.

Jennifer Garner cute?

Jennifer Aniston cute. Tom looks at Simone, eyebrows raised like she should be impressed. *Friends* era, he adds.

What do you need me for?

She's not twenty-one.

Simone hits him with her pillow. Why did you bring your son for ice cream by my place?

It was a coincidence.

Oh. I thought maybe. Simone does not dare look at Tom's face. The Mike's Hard Lemonade face, she's sure.

I won't leave my wife.

I know. You should go.

What am I supposed to do for an hour?

Fifty-five minutes.

Did I say something?

You make the cat nervous.

I always stay until nine.

She claws up all my shoes. I have to hide them when you're over.

Because I said my wife is cute?

If she would have sex with you, would you be here?

Of course not.

Oh. Simone rolls herself into her quilt and away from Tom. A little wall-facing pink burrito. It came out of his mouth so easily. She isn't even worth a lie.

Tom stays on his back, hands in his hair. His ginger-root fingers. The three Slinkys of chest hair. His wet-dog smell. His wispy orgasmic grunt, like an eighty-year-old man who's crossed the finish line of a marathon he should've never entered. His wife, his child. But all he needs to do is say one reassuring thing. You are *Friends*-era Jennifer Aniston cute. I admire your vast knowledge of fashion trends and celebrity news. Your highlights are well integrated. You have great running form.

Fine, he says. I'll go.

Fine. Go.

Thanks for all the sex.

Say hi to your wife for me.

Tom leaves. Simone folds herself in half and cries. She thought she held the power, she was the saviour. How did she end up worse off than him—emptier, lonelier? Will she have to quit running group?

* * *

At 8:30 p.m. Tom rings the doorbell. Meg stares at him from their bedroom window. It occurs to her she could leave him there, change the locks, toss his subscription to *Runner's World* on the front lawn. She could keep Sebastian hostage inside. Tom would eventually give up. He'd go live with that running bunny he's fucking. The lady from the ice cream parlour Sebastian told her about.

But then Meg would be a single mother, an untouchable. She'd be alone and possibly lonelier than she is now. Now she has a five-year-old boy's selfish love, as it should be, and the love of a thirty-year-old man who has no idea how selfish he is. No idea what he calls love is only possession, his acts of kindness are laced with expectation. His margins swarm with greedy, insatiable need. Even Tom's eyes feel like an imposition on her personal space. Meg grasps stubbornly at anything of her own, anything pre-Tom: Sleater-Kinney CDs, photos of old boyfriends, time. When it is given, an hour to herself, she seeps it through her hands like play clay, unsure of her ability to form it. She's walked two blocks from home only to curl to the sidewalk and cry into her sleeves, return to bed before twenty minutes have passed. Meg entered this marriage for protection and procreation. She thought she could coast, content. But here she is, replete with unmarked desire. For anything but this black hole, those hands that grab and take from her, those mouths that ask *of*, but not *about* her.

Tom looks helpless out there in his tights and nylon jacket. He cradles both elbows, nods to the neighbours, pushes the bell again. He'll wake Sebastian.

Lost your key?

I did, actually.

How does that happen?

I keep it in my running shoes. It must have slipped out.

You're home early.

I came home as soon as I realized. About the key.

If you realized, why didn't you stop and look for it?

I realized later.

How did you realize, if it was later?

Can I come in?

Meg removes her arm from where it rested against the door jamb, pivots her legs to create space for her husband and extends an arm of welcome. It's your house.

It's yours too.

Is it?

God, Meg. Tom tosses his jacket to the floor.

Is it over, then?

Running?

Fucking.

What?

Meg picks up the jacket, hooks it to their coat rack. Sorry. Maybe you're in love. The lovemaking, then.

I need it from someone, Meg.

This would be the time to touch him. Not a shuffle-past in the hall, but to touch him. To save her marriage, like a drowning puppy or an allowance. To crack herself open like a dry-glued paperback. To moan for him in her highest octave. To rip off his skin and wear him like a cloak. But she would rather do this with anyone—the mop-headed barista who makes phallic art in her lattes, the silver-haired children's librarian with the low V-necks and high boots—than Tom. To do so would be to lose control. Sebastian took her body and she cannot pass it back to Tom. She clings to the only tangible expression of herself. A fight for freedom she doesn't have the guts to put into words.

*　*　*

When Mommy takes Sebastian to swimming lessons, she makes sure he wears his swimsuit under his clothes so it's not such a rush. She remembers to bring fresh underwears for after. She sits at the edge of the pool with a towel and hugs him up when class is over. She lets him put his wet hand under her shirt and squeeze her squishy tummy.

I eat you, Mommy. Eat means love. I eat you.

I eat you too.

Mommy kisses Sebastian's head and says, Let's get ice cream. She takes him to the faraway place by the ocean. She lets him put on as many toppings as he wants. Daddy always gives him a maximilium. Your maximilium is two. One sweet, one healthy.

Mommy asks Sebastian, Is this where you met Daddy's friend?

What friend?

The lady with the shiny legs.

Spiny legs?

You told me Daddy had a friend with shiny pink legs.

Daddy's friend Simone?

Is this where you met her?

Yup.

Sebastian's ice cream has all sorts of sprinkles. Chocolate, strawberry, multicoloured sprinkles. And cherries. Caramel sauce. Marshmallows.

I wonder if she'll come in today.

What, Mommy?

Simone.

There's a puppy. Sebastian reaches his arm out to the window.

Mommy wants to stay at the ice cream store for a long time. Longer than Sebastian has to sit still on the Sharing Carpet at kindergarten. Longer than he has to sit very, very still with the bowl on his head for Daddy and the scissors. Sebastian ate all his toppings. Only gooey-dribbledy-mush is left.

Can we go home now?

You didn't finish your ice cream.

It's all shlurpy.

Sebastian reaches up for Mommy's hand but she says, Sometimes Mommy gets tired of dragging you around. She puts her hand in her pocket.

Outside the ice cream store, Sebastian sees Daddy's friend Simone. Sebastian stretches his arm to the sky and opens and closes his hand. He says, Hallo Simone.

Daddy's friend Simone turns her head. She stands still. She waves to Sebastian.

Mommy doesn't say anything. She puts both hands on Sebastian's shoulders like she does when they're near a busy road. Sebastian jumps up and down. Daddy's friend Simone and Mommy are both very still.

* * *

Her name is Skye. Tom is certain Meg chose this therapist because her website is spattered with vaginal art—bearded irises and cocoons. This charade will surely end with an exchange of raw chocolate recipes. Skye floats around her office in a white parachute of a dress. Meg inhabits the miniskirt she bought four years ago when she and Tom dressed as Tennis Ken and Barbie for Halloween. That miniskirt has enveloped Meg's midsection more often than not lately. Tom can't help but feel responsible. When she sits, a little triangle of panty is visible between her thighs but their relationship is such, at the moment, that Meg's spinach in the teeth, undone flies and peekaboo panties are best left to her own discovery.

Why don't you tell me why you're here today? Skye drifts into her chair.

He cheated on me.

Thank you, Meg. I meant what feeling-state has brought you here?

Betrayal?

Fair enough. Tom?

I feel that she hasn't touched me in nine months.

What about the Thompsons' Christmas party?

You called me Ethan.

You're all about the fucking details.

I hear that Tom feels frustrated. Would you agree, Meg?

Are you blaming me?

Skye clasps her hands. Tilts her head at Meg and Tom in turn. She says, The affair happened. There's no one to blame.

I'm pretty sure there is.

What is it like for you, Meg, when you and Tom are intimate?

Meg is silent for a long time. Minutes. Tom is embarrassed in front of Skye, in front of any woman, anyone. Tom thinks about how this will cost him $1.33 per minute not to mention the babysitting fees and Meg has wasted approximately seven dollars in silence.

Like. Meg looks up toward the *Affirming Messages* mobile on the ceiling. Like, I don't know. Like I'm being molested by my high school PE teacher.

Skye's face sucks into itself and quickly recovers into eyebrows-united, squiggle-mouthed understanding.

Molested? I'm your husband.

I know you're attractive. Meg air-quotes the word *attractive*. She looks at Tom but he holds her in his periphery. But, she says, it makes me sick to fold your laundry.

I could do the laundry, Tom mumbles.

To touch these things that have touched you.

Tom strokes Meg's knee. I'm sorry about Simone.

Meg looks at his hand, and then up, straight-faced. This isn't about her.

I don't understand.

Meg grabs two fistfuls of hair, pulls it in front of her eyes. This doesn't feel like my real life.

What about my real life? And Sebastian's?

Meg lifts her head to meet Tom's, her eyes wide now, not with pity but horror. She says, I'm living *your* lives.

You're a wife and mother, Meg. You chose this.

Skye lifts her index finger to her lips. Let's hear Meg's story, she says.

This is all bullshit, Tom says. And he means *all* of it. The therapist named after a conglomerate of air, Meg's selfishness, his sex life, his marriage.

* * *

Tom's key sulks in a corner of Simone's galley kitchen, where her cat coughed it up last week. For a week, Simone has key-stared, inhaled strawberry ice cream, plotted revenge. She's been ditched by players for being only one woman, by possessive introverts for being too much woman, but never by an old man for being the wrong woman. This was not supposed to happen. Sugar-high, Simone forms a giddy plan. She'll let herself in through the back while Tom's at running group. Breathe the recirculated air of his married life. Lie on his bed. Leave the key in his sock drawer. Steal his wife's perfume then wear it to running group to mess with him. Play the thwarted mistress, but without the bloody death scene.

Nobody's home. If Tom's family went missing tonight, the crime scene investigators would report they'd left in a panic. A pot carpeted with tangled spaghetti soaks in the sink. The dishwasher is open, the bottom rack rolled out like a diseased tongue. There's a bright-yellow field trip permission form on the kitchen table. Burnt toast crumbs and curly brown hairs gather around a dried-up milk puddle on the floor underneath. Simone gags a little. She fingers the key. She could throw it to the floor, a victim of the sticky milk hole. Tomorrow at breakfast Tom's family would laugh—*That's where we left the key!*—Tom and his wife would pinch their son's cheeks. Life would go on.

What the fucking shit?

Simone gasps. Throws the key toward Tom's wife in the dark living room. Runs.

Ow! Hey! Stop!

Simone does not stop. She's a runner. Tom's wife grabs the collar of her jean jacket.

Get out of my house.

I'm trying to.

Tom's wife pulls her into the back entryway then releases her. Simone leans against the wall, rests her head against a coat peg.

I want to squish your little face, Tom's wife says through her teeth.

I'm sorry.

Deflate you.

I never thought about, like, Tom's world.

Don't say his name. He's not yours. Tom's wife steps around Simone, into the kitchen. She lifts herself up on the counter, flips through the newspaper by the gloomy orange light of a streetlamp outside, *hmm*s at the fashion section, creates psychopathic tension. She raises her head and asks, Was it a forbidden fruit thing or was it him?

Simone flaps her lips. She slides her hands into the back pockets of her stretch jeans and says, It's never really him.

Someday you'll realize all the lives you've fucked with.

*　*　*

Meg thinks about what she could do with the key before Tom returns. She could place it on his pillow. They could fight about Simone. She could say I can't believe you fucked a woman who wears baby-blue eyeliner. She could string it around her neck—a latchkey excuse for her anger, apathy, abstinence.

Simone cries and apologizes in Meg's back entryway. Meg hears a few words through the bubbly mucous, like *dirty whore, self-esteem, Angelina Jolie.*

Forget it, Meg says. She pats Simone's shoulder. If it wasn't you it'd be some other—

Simone snorkels into her sleeve. Is this what marriage is like?

My marriage.

You just stop?

He could be asking me to make him a peanut butter sandwich.

I'm never getting married.

But, incessantly.

I felt like a sex toy.

Meg exhales damply. I didn't need to hear that. She stares into her lap then up at Simone. Beyond the push-up bra, bleached hair and eye makeup, Simone is a plain girl. Meg feels both insulted and validated by this.

Simone says, Well I should—

The doorknob turns. Tom pushes the door open and stands, spread-legged and sweaty in the doorway.

Don't drip on the mat, Meg says.

You're—Tom points at Simone.

I'll go.

We were talking, Meg says.

Great, Tom says. The mat now more sweat than fibre.

She brought your key. Meg points to the living room where the key landed. She threw it at me.

Tom looks stunned, then sympathetic, then stunned again. He walks toward the key, turns to Meg. Did she get you?

Meg tugs at the neck of her shirt. Grazed my shoulder.

Bad shot.

Tom steps closer to Meg.

Meg tightens her shoulders, then relaxes.

Tom fingers a small, slow ring around her wound.

Simone repeats, I'll go.

Tom looks away from Meg, raises his hand from Meg's shoulder to bid farewell to Simone.

*   *   *

Sebastian dreams he's at a jumbled-up swimming lesson. He's in the pool in his underwears with a towel tight into his face. The pool is full of shlurpy ice cream with snapping caramel eels. Sebastian feels like there's a marshmallow in his throat when he wakes up. He can't talk or hardly breathe. He runs to Mommy and Daddy's room but there's no soft lump on Mommy's side of the bed. He hears Mommy's voice and creeps toward the wall between the toilet and the kitchen like he does when screamy voices wake him up. He hears Mommy talk about peanut butter sandwiches and he feels hungry. Mommy and Daddy talk in their inside voices. Maybe Mommy is making Daddy a peanut butter sandwich. Daddy probably licked the peanut-buttery knife because he says, I'm sorry, to Mommy. Mommy says, I can't. She must be frust-er-ated with the lid. She must be really frust-er-ated because she starts to cry. Maybe she'll have a temper. It must be a really tricky lid because Daddy tells Mommy, There's nothing more we can do.

What Is Good

The first thing Gwen noticed about Celeste was the funnel cloud of blonde hair tied atop her head with a ragged fuchsia ribbon—binding ripped from her daughter's dress or the collar of a runaway show dog. No, that's a lie. The first thing Gwen noticed was the smell of booze that preceded her. Booze on her breath, booze that swarmed her and seeped from her pores.

It was the year after Meg left her husband and moved into that fourplex for single-parent families with her son. It overlooked a park full of plum trees whose trunks propped up young rakish bodies with haggard faces. The Heartbreak Hotel, Meg called it. When Gwen came over to babysit Sebastian, the children of the building would roam the park in thick-soled shoes with strict orders to avoid needles and desiccated sofas. Their mothers sat at a picnic table out front and bitched about child support, restraining orders and the selection of available men—all either mid-twenties who thought an episiotomy was a body shot and single motherhood was "badass" or mid-forties and encumbered with guilt, erectile dysfunction and batshit-crazy ex-wives.

Celeste seemed ageless. Crow's feet of a fifty-year-old, smooth throat of a twenty-year-old, giggle of a ten-year-old. She plunked a paper bag in front of Gwen and Sebastian, unaware of the game of checkers she'd ruffled, and handed her young daughter— her halfling pale shadow, a rag doll crowned by hair the blinding shade of blonde only children can have, following silently at arm's length like a stray cat—the key to her place.

Heya, Simon, Celeste said to Gwen's grandson. Celeste's eyes were near clear, like tap water, like there was not enough iris to render them blue. And her pupils the blurry seeping lethargy brought by a Scotch, neat. A vodka screwdriver. A pitcher of sangria.

He's Sebastian. Gwen extended a hand. I'm Gwen.

Meg's sister?

I love you already.

Just moved in. Celeste, she said. And little Louisa. She gestured to the girl, now two-stepping down the porch stairs, hands braided around a dark glass of iced tea, cubes clinking like rocks in rum.

I'm Meg's mother. I watch Sebastian a couple nights a week.

He looks about Louisa's age. You two should play. Celeste urged her daughter by the shoulder toward Sebastian. Louisa sat at Sebastian's feet and dipped her head into her glass.

Your turn, Grandma. Grandma, your turn. Sebastian tugged at Gwen's sleeve.

Gwen retracted her arm. Sorry buddy, she said. She focused on her grandson, the game. She twisted her lips up. But there was that click in her throat, the squeeze, the emptiness, like it had never left her. She hopped a black plastic circle over two of his reds and pressed them into her palm.

Sebastian's lips quivered.

Was I supposed to let you win?

He shook his head. He edged a red forward, impulsive, created a gap. Gwen breathed, one, two. In, out. She knew the right
thing to do. Let the boy win, smile at him with her eyes, go inside
and make cookies. Let him spill flour, crush eggshells into the
batter, dip fingers from nostril to dough. But there was the wanting, the relentless wanting she'd tamed every second of every day
for the few months she'd been sober. And the boy, the reason for
the sobriety, the wanting, the reason the wanting was wanting
and not having, and she suddenly resented him.

So when Celeste ran up the steps to her place and returned
with two glasses of iced tea, and when she reached into her paper
bag and pulled out a bottle of vodka, and when she winked at
Gwen and said, Happy mom, happy kids, and dumped vodka
into the glasses, Gwen said yes. Just like that. As though the
only thing keeping her sober was that nobody had bothered to
ask. And because of the way the strap of Celeste's dress strolled
off her shoulder, the way she never once tried to right it, and the
way Louisa circled her mother, groped at her as if Celeste's body
was her own, even the way the excessive flesh hung from Celeste's
bones—it seemed the entire world hinged from Celeste and she
couldn't care less.

Gwen said yes to one glass because it was almost spring and
spring was made for hard iced tea. Nothing wrong with one
glass. Nothing wrong with vodka in the springtime. Vodka and a
picnic table. Who wouldn't partake? And then yes to two glasses.
Celeste was French and in France no one judges you for drinking.
In France where they're progressive, France where they're chic.
And yes to three glasses, when Gwen loved everyone and everyone loved her. She belonged everywhere. How could she have
anything but love for the boy? Sebastian watching TV or whatever

the hell he was doing at Celeste's place with Louisa, such a good boy. And wasn't Gwen laughing now and wasn't that good? And wasn't Sebastian making a new friend and weren't childhood memories made of the times spent away from adult supervision? Wouldn't he have so many stories to tell? Wouldn't he become such an interesting person?

Gwen awoke on the floor, out of breath, beside a thin smear of puke, like hardened beeswax on the carpet. She recognized the carpet as hers. Jeans and blouse from the day before. She remembered agonizing the previous morning over the ruffle of pink, the low neckline. Was she one of those thin old ladies in miniskirts with turkey necks who thought they were fooling somebody? Would Meg disapprove?

Gwen checked her phone. A text from Meg: *That was highly inappropriate.*

Gwen remembered nothing highly inappropriate. Nothing past the picnic table. Highly inappropriate was good. Highly inappropriate meant she had stayed until Meg returned home. It meant she hadn't caused Sebastian's death—mutilation by whipper snapper, third-degree burns from the frozen pizza he'd had to heat in the oven himself, kidnapping by a responsible-looking passerby. She would leave it at highly inappropriate. She would not do this again. Never again. She would not drink. She hadn't, really. She was meeting a neighbour for the first time. She was fine. She was still sober. Still different. Not the same old Gwen.

Same old Gwen would say fuck everyone and drink herself right back to sleep. Same old Gwen would end up without Meg. Alone-alone, the way she'd been before Meg and Tom split, before Meg went to school Wednesday and Friday evenings, before Meg was so desperate for help she forgave *the incident* and called her. Mom, I need you. Are you sober?

Gwen said yes, and it was not a lie. She held intentions of sobriety. She became sober. Soon as she hung up the phone. Mostly sober. Boring, monstrous, sober. Gwen had to remind herself of this reason for doing what is good rather than what feels good. What feels good leads to alone-alone.

That Friday after school, Gwen held Sebastian's sticky fingers between hers. His wide eyes on her, the unknowing love she used to receive from men. But the worst thing about a man was the best thing about a child. She wanted to be that thing Sebastian loved. That warm, gooey mother figure, buoyed by the downward tug of dependence. The physics of it made no sense to her. Perhaps to no one. Perhaps all the other women were better at fooling.

Sebastian let go of her hand and walked in a swizzling zigzag, at times in front of her, at times behind, stepping on her toes, in front of her toes, stopping at every parking meter to push every button. Had her girls been so swirly and entitled? Did one walk home require so much deep breathing?

At Dad's house, on Saturdays, we play Mario Kart.

Mmm.

Dad's special friend Sunny won the Banana Cup last time.

Sunny?

Sometimes she has a sleepover. And we have bacon in the morning.

Your mom wouldn't want you eating bacon.

This isn't the way home, Grandma.

We're going a little farther. I need to get something for Celeste.

Sometimes I play with Louisa.

Is she nice?

She has an elephant stuffy.

Let's get a gift for Celeste and one for someone in my building. He's having a party.

Celeste has lots of parties.

Does she?

She has lots of those. Sebastian poked the mickey of vodka Gwen stuffed into her purse.

When Gwen and Sebastian arrived, Celeste sat atop the picnic table outside Meg's building, legs spread wide, framing an array of tarot cards. A deep-purple sarong covered her body, wrapped around her neck and draped from right above her nipples to right below her hips, an affront to the very idea of private parts. Her bare legs like Jell-O salad with kneecap islands, her breasts drooped over her ribs. She was raw and feral, dug from the bowels of the earth, a fleshy essence.

Gwen, she yelled in greeting. Crazy night Wednesday, eh?

Gwen nodded.

You have an amazing singing voice. Real husky.

Thanks. Gwen maintained eye contact with the picnic table. She had a vague memory of a Lady Gaga air guitar performance. Most likely on top of the picnic table. Possibly with costumes and a stage dive, which would explain the greenish purple bruise creeping up her thigh.

Louisa was hunched on all fours under the picnic table, scraping her fingers through the soil. Sebastian dropped his backpack and crouched.

Whatcha doing?

Making ant paths.

Gwen, let's do your tarot. Celeste gathered the cards in her hands.

I should get dinner started.

Dinner? God, we're living off frozen pizza and apples.

Gotta keep up Meg's standards.

She's always stirring some pot full of green.

I'm more of a Kraft Dinner girl, Gwen said.

We'll break her eventually.

Here. Gwen plunged an arm into her bag until it hit cold plastic. For the other day. Thanks. She handed the mickey of vodka to Celeste.

You one hundred percent didn't have to.

I know, but... Gwen dropped the bottle between Celeste's legs and headed up the steps to Meg's door. Sebastian followed her in, slinked to his room and emerged with the checkerboard dragging behind him like a security blanket. He said nothing but looked up at Gwen with tentative expectation.

Not today, bud.

But we always.

Why don't you play with Louisa?

Sebastian nodded, left the board on the floor and walked back outside.

Hey, Gwen shouted. And then muttered, Could you put away...

Sebastian didn't hear. He was under the picnic table, knuckles-deep in soil.

Inside, Gwen sliced eggplant. Meg had left a list: Dinner at 5:00 – Eggplant Parmesan p. 373 Joy of Cooking / Please bathe Sebastian (make him wash armpits and bum, hair wash not necessary) / Make sure he brushes teeth for two minutes /

Bed at 7:30 – read from schoolbook for at least fifteen mins. No comics / p.s. he can play with Louisa but you should stay away from Celeste.

Gwen sliced. *Thin slices*, the cookbook said. Her slices were paper thin. Look how well she followed instructions. Her slices fainted over one another like dominoes. Look at this poor eggplant. Look at what Meg made her do to it. And look at how well she stayed away from Celeste. One hundred eggplant slices away, at least. And how well she was not drinking. She had spent two days not drinking. She had bought vodka and not drunk it. She had vodka in her purse and she was not drinking it. Not drinking, not drinking, not drinking. Not being alone-alone. So she could have Meg. Bossy, unappreciative Meg who made her slice eggplants and cut her finger so it bled all over her slices. Gwen sucked the blood from her finger. Reached for her purse. Swore there was a Band-Aid in there somewhere. Sebastian hated eggplant anyway. Everyone did.

Gwen brought the extra mickey of vodka from her purse out to the picnic table and said, Got any iced tea?

Celeste, legs open around a pitcher of cranberry juice, took the vodka from Gwen and poured it in. No dinner? she said.

Eggplant parmesan.

Yuck.

I abandoned it.

What would Meg say?

She told me to stay away from you.

She told me the same thing. Celeste handed the pitcher to Gwen, who cradled it with her bottom lip, let its contents flow down her throat until she gagged. She sat between Celeste's thighs and drank pitchers and pitchers of cranberry juice. Celeste piled Gwen's hair, thin and straw-scratchy from years of dye—layers of red so mutated it shone bright purple in the sun—atop her head and stuck it with a sweat-dripped bobby pin retrieved from her cleavage. Gwen drank so her head felt heavy with hair, thick and shiny and naturally coloured. And her legs felt smooth and invisibly veined, her feet bunion-free, toenails Passionfruit Pink, and her stomach and cunt were tight, unstretched by any human life forms other than all the cocks of all the guys. She laughed and laughed and told Celeste about when she was twenty-one and met Meg's father, Damian, the lead singer of a punk band. About how good it felt to be attached to him, to punk rock, a movement that revered the unlikeable. To want Damian, who wanted nothing but solitude with a dash of reverence—an unachievable goal, consequence-free striving. A frenetic beat. A moment. No future.

Cheers to that, said Celeste. But why waste our breath on men? Forget men. Forget anyone who wants anything from you.

And Sebastian and Louisa buzzed around the picnic table where Gwen and Celeste sat and ran in and out of Celeste's place with bags of chips and chocolate cookies while Meg's dissected eggplant slouched on her counter. And Gwen slid into the jelly under Celeste's ribs, farther and farther until she wasn't sure Celeste was human at all and not made of vodka.

What happened to my eggplant?

Gwen opened her eyes. Meg's cheeks hung over her.

What did you feed Sebastian?

Celeste fed the kids.

You were with Celeste?

No.

You just said.

I meant I fed him. Me.

What happened with the eggplant?

I sliced it very thin.

What happened to you?

Gwen rubbed her eyes. Assessed her surroundings. Warm, breathing lump, stuffies, Pokémon cards. Sebastian's mattress. We fell asleep, Gwen said.

Did you read stories?

Meg. All these questions first thing in the morning.

It's ten o'clock at night.

It's still Friday?

Mom, are you?

I'm not. I haven't. A few drinks. I'm not *drinking*.

You had drinks?

No. I meant she did. I didn't.

Please stay away from her.

You can't control me.

You can't control yourself.

I'm not like you, Meg.

I know. I know you're not.

Gwen closed her eyes. She held Meg's hand, and Meg squeezed her fingers. Meg would stop squeezing when pity turned to frustration, annoyance. When *I'm not like you* meant I reside on the other side of the line you've drawn in order to make sense of your world. And to understand my side would require untying all the knots in the rope you've groped to arrive at yours.

Mom, I need you.

On Saturday, Gwen remained sober. She woke up and drank tea. She watched TV until one of the characters had a glass of wine. She turned off the TV. She stared at the wall. She stared out the window. She listened to her neighbour cough. She made some more tea. She would go to the beach. She would exfoliate her heels in sand and allow the waves to crash over her and visualize her future. Her future, in which she would meet a rich, older American gentleman who had anchored his yacht in the bay. He had lost his wife to cancer and was looking for an exotic Canadian who had all her original teeth and whose ass had only dropped an inch or so. They would sail around the world and drink margaritas moderately and she would teach him the nicknames for her currency and about ketchup chips and the Trudeaus until she slid into death among a commune of mermaids. His name would be John. He would be simple in name and nature and in need of the excitement only a slightly unhinged woman could offer. These things could still happen. Gwen was in her late fifties. That was practically a teenager to a seventy-year-old man not rich enough to attract a twenty-year-old, but enough to afford a steady supply of Viagra.

Gwen made it one block before her body tugged her in the direction of a liquor store. *The beach is this way*, she told her legs. There's a liquor store two blocks to the right. It won't take long. Everyone brings coolers to the beach. Teenagers do it. Teenagers aren't alcoholics. And wouldn't drinking like a teenager make her feel like a teenager? And she had John to consider. How could she make interesting conversation with him if her head was saying *don't drink don't drink don't drink* the whole time? Coolers at the beach were imperative to her future. And a mickey of vodka for when she returned home and might need help sleeping after all the good times. Doctors' wives drank a glass of wine to help them sleep, she'd seen it on her soaps. How different was this?

Gwen found a smooth log in the intermediate area of the beach—past the shallows where smug young families dug moats, and before the curve of the bay where the tide went far out leaving stretches of sand on which teenagers mastered volleyballs and skimboards. To her left, a nude leathery man asleep in the crotch of a driftwood shack, and to her right, a white-haired woman dressed in a pilling red sweatsuit, hand-feeding bread crumbs to the seagulls. Gwen cracked a cooler and guzzled. She hadn't brought a container to conceal her alcohol. No one would notice her anyway.

Fuck you, young families splishing and splashing and Daddy this and Mommy that-ing. How did you become so boring? You probably had pancakes for breakfast—from scratch with organic maple syrup. You probably bought a bag of Cheetos on your way to the beach. You probably ate them all in one go and felt really sinful. You probably work for the government writing reports about report writing. You probably own a hanger for your ties. You probably wear a Garfield tie on casual Friday and think you're pretty fucking whimsical. And fuck you, teenagers shrieking and frolicking and—*Oops! Hahaha! Stop it!*—nippling out of your skimpy, weather-inappropriate bikinis. Enjoy it while it lasts, suckers. Your tits'll hang past your cunt soon enough. Get those boys' attention now—in thirty years they'll make you invisible. Gwen raised a cooler to the teenagers' side of the bay and shouted, I'll keep this seat warm for you, bitches!

By Wednesday, Gwen had drunk herself to sleep four nights in a row and every cashier at every liquor store within a five-block radius of her apartment eyed her in the way one would address a recurring cold sore. A slide show of the last few days' activities sporadically interrupted her thoughts: rubbing sunscreen on a pair of acned shoulders caped with tufts of dark hair;

hyperventilating into an empty chip bag; swearing to her neighbour that she lived in 4B, that she'd always lived in 4B, there was no way her neighbour lived in 4B because it was hers, then realizing 4A felt more like home. If it weren't for Meg's text message that morning reminding her it was Sebastian's last day of school before spring break, she would have no idea where to place herself along the rest of the world's timeline.

At school, the parents ignored her. Gwen sat on a bench beside Sad Single Dad who wore a lime-green golf shirt and a lazy moustache. He moved a foot away from her. Gwen scanned herself. Shirt, yes. Buttons in their proper holes. Fly high, shoes tied. She discreetly nosed an armpit. It had the cozy funk of morning after. An odour that could only evoke fond memories. Unless you were hard up. She turned to Sad Single Dad. Is that it? she said.

What?

Are you hard up?

Excuse me?

You moved away from me.

Sad Single Dad looked down at the bench and said, I thought you'd need more room for your bag.

Gwen noticed the backup mickey of vodka poking out from her purse. Oh, my baaaag, she said.

Sad Single Dad looked at the classroom door, then at the clock.

Do you have a problem with my bag?

Sad Single Dad stared at the clock.

Do you have a problem with this? Gwen pulled out her mickey of vodka and held it up to Sad Single Dad's face. Do you have a problem with someone having a party later? Should a grandmother not have friends?

It's fine, Sad Single Dad said.

The school bell rang. Kids stormed the halls. I'm having a party later, Gwen mumbled. When she spotted Sebastian, she yelled, Hey buddy!

Sebastian looked up, raised a hand to Gwen, and retreated to the cloakroom.

On the walk home, Gwen reached for Sebastian's hand but he slid it away to push the crosswalk button and then clung to the straps of his backpack. Gwen had been snubbed by a man before. She could play this game. She put her hands in her pockets and gave Sebastian one-word answers the rest of the way.

When she and Sebastian approached Meg's building, he ran straight to Celeste's door without bothering to ask Gwen for a game of checkers. Celeste sat at the picnic table holding a glass of wine up to Gwen. Gwen's stomach turned. They were like tired lovers in a seedy motel room. Past seduction into the slump of assumption. Gwen noticed now the aggressive jag of Celeste's canines, as though they were plummeting toward the tip of her tongue. Her fingers, yellow and slender, too slender to fit with her robust frame, made her seem not dainty but arachnid. And her smell, the sterile tang of vodka, yes, but now laced with the sweet funk of unwashed feet and sun-soaked dog shit.

These qualities were once attractive to Gwen in their deviation from the sober reality she consistently tried, and failed, to subscribe to. Meg's reality. Had Gwen's disciplinary techniques ever achieved the perfect balance between doormat and dictator? Had she ever followed a recipe to completion? Had she ever read *Alligator Pie* as intended, allowing for improvisation while maintaining rhythm and tone? She never had and never would and neither would Meg. But it was okay for Meg to fail because she made the rules and it was okay for Celeste to fail because she didn't even try. Gwen rested somewhere in between. Gwen floated in a rubber dinghy inside a half-empty bottle of vodka, watching others succeed at failing and failing to succeed. And all she could do was dip in her straw and not think too much.

Come on, Gwen. My arm hurts. Celeste raised Gwen's glass of wine.

Gwen didn't take it. Don't you get tired of this?

You sound like Meg.

Meg's got it together.

She can toss a salad.

Meg depends on nobody.

Except you.

You think she knows I'm drinking?

Celeste shrugged. Any friend of mine...

I've stopped promising myself I'll quit.

Nothing wrong with a drink or two.

I lost Sebastian once. I passed out and lost him.

But you found him.

Meg found him.

Kids are resilient. Meg's too uptight.

Something good could still happen. I should be sober for it.

This is something good.

I want to meet a rich man, live on a yacht.

Then what?

Gwen stared at the glass of wine.

Sebastian poked his head from Celeste's doorway, his little fingers tucked into the crack of the door, resting atop a hinge. Grandma, he said. Can I have a Mr. Freeze? Just this once?

Gwen ran to him. Sebastian, she yelled, and grabbed his hand. Your fingers could get slammed in the door, she said. They could fall off. She wrapped her arms around the boy, pulled his body close to hers.

Grandma, Sebastian puffed. It's squishy.

A Mr. Freeze is a toxic rainbow, Gwen said. It's dangerous in there.

Can I go back? Sebastian looked back at Louisa, now in the doorway. Louisa staring wide and unfocused at the world outside.

Gwen squeezed Sebastian's hand. Let's go home, she said. Let's play checkers.

I want to play with Louisa.

Don't you love Grandma?

We were watching TV. I want a Mr. Freeze. Mom doesn't let me do that stuff.

Gwen tugged Sebastian's arm toward Meg's door. Remember when we used to play checkers?

Meg returned to Gwen and Sebastian on the living room floor, fists full of popcorn and playing cards. Gwen drank a glass of orange juice, spiked with a splash of emergency vodka to take the edge off. To ease into sobriety. Because she would become sober.

Brush your teeth, Meg said to Sebastian. Bedtime was an hour ago.

We had fun, didn't we Sebbie? Gwen said.

Sebastian nodded, stood and hugged his mother's leg.

Did you have any dinner? Meg asked.

Popcorn, Sebastian said.

Homemade, Gwen said. And grapes. Green ones.

Meg nodded. Thanks, Mom.

I guess I should've made a salad.

Meg pressed her lips together, poked the corners of her mouth into her cheeks. Perhaps the way she smiled at Tom before they split, when he'd apologize for staying late at running group.

When he'd joke with her about the young female runners—the garish colour of their sneakers, their immodest sports bras—feigning disapproval for the chance to speak of them, for the thrill of feeling their features grace his tongue.

Meg dipped her head in a slow nod and said, You do your best.

When Gwen left, Celeste sat at the picnic table with Gwen's glass beside her, full and untouched. She drank from her glass steadily, rhythmically. Same beat, same three chords. Red wine, gin, vodka.

Go ahead and drink mine, Gwen said.

Celeste raised Gwen's glass and complied. She wouldn't be there long. Celeste was the mundane frenetic. A steady beat that wouldn't slow for the world around her. The future of no future. Inside Celeste's open apartment door, the glow of the TV broken by her future—little Louisa, inanimate and impossibly light blonde.

Tom's Wedding

What did you expect, here in your little black dress? When the invitation arrived, red-speckled like debris from a gory car crash, you trashed it. How dare they? But here you are, having scratched off globs of hardened banana from the card stock to make out the address. The bigger person. Curious. Self-destructive. Tom's wedding is outdoors, tented like a circus. Pity about the ominous rain clouds. Did they stay up all night making pinwheels to line the walk? Did they make up rhymes to decorate their place settings? *We fit together like clothes and peg: Tom and Meg.* No, they did not. Her name is Sunny. Sunny does not rhyme with peg.

And there he is, slightly hunched (apprehensive?), under an arch dripping with pink and white carnations—*carnations*—in his tux, handsome as always, but unsexed now, like a kindergarten teacher. He's a little bulky to look good in a tux. This man could've killed you in your sleep. And here you sit, in the miscellaneous section next to his barber and barista, tugging at the hem of your dress. When plotting wardrobe you forgot this is not a sitting dress. Luckily, no one here knows who you are. Tom's new life, Tom's new friends. Your old couple friends stopped calling either of you after the divorce. There is no greater threat to the institution of marriage than a defector at one's dinner party.

You introduce yourself to the barber as Tom's masseuse. He likes it rough, you say.

He likes a close shave, the barber says.

You cross your legs toward the barber. He's cute. Pomades sparingly. More appropriate for you than Chad, the waifish twenty-two-year-old you met a few weeks ago at the library. Chad claimed to be studying linguistics, but when you asked if he'd read any good Chomsky and he said either *No?* or *Noam?* you didn't push. When you frequent his cereal-crumbed futon, Chad touches you tentatively, like a Braille reader, like he's afraid to break you. You did not bring Chad today because boyfriends escort people to weddings. You don't have boyfriends. You are a strong, independent woman. No need to marry the first thing that comes along.

Your conversation with Tom's barber about the comeback of carnations is interrupted by Pachelbel's Canon. You turn to him and whisper, Original, followed by a snort. Yes, a snort, a loud one, at Tom's wedding, and you know he'll know whose nose and throat it emanated from because he knows you that well and you slap your cheek and ear and shake your head to stop your thoughts from edging toward missing him, someone you felt comfortable enough to snort with, and realize on account of the snorting and self-hitting you have ruined any chances of bagging the barber.

Sunny strolls down the aisle in a tiered strapless satin number, like an aged Anne Geddes baby swallowed by a hydrangea. She couldn't be more different from you. Obviously a rebound. Because you were so right for him. What were those six years of your life about, then? You still don't know what he saw in you. Someone willing to take him on. Maybe that's all it is. Someone insecure enough to believe they deserve you at your worst. Someone to hold your hand at other people's weddings. Clearly, you are above all this. You're the winner.

Sebastian sits up front beside Tom's mother. Here in his little black suit. It makes sense he's not with you. He's here for Tom. This isn't your day. You don't like the way Tom's mother hovers over Sebastian, nitpicking. Moving his hands into his lap, brushing his hairs back into place, licking her finger and smudging peanut butter from the side of his mouth. She barely knows him. She didn't make the trip from Ottawa to attend your wedding. Some sort of work emergency. You've met her a total of three times.

Sebastian looks back and you catch his eye, wave, force a smile. He waves back, forces a smile. Pity? Pity. From your seven-year-old son. The things he's come to understand. Transition days, Mom's house, Dad's house, special friends, girlfriends, second weddings. That love could be anything but unconditional. Does he worry you will stop loving him too? You want to run over and hold him. Tell him you do still love his father. You do. If only he weren't such an asshole. But you're here. How could you not be? To refuse the invitation would be to admit you're hurt. And you're not. You are happy for him. Him and Sunny. Tom and Sunny. Sunny and Tom. Sunny and Tom. Sunny and Tom.

Sunny and Tom say *I do* and everyone cheers and Tom unveils his bride. You want to yell, Surprise! but nobody here would get your joke. You don't even get your joke. Despite your best interests, you watch them kiss. How cute, the way she reveals her tongue before slithering it between his lips. What brings bile to your throat is the way he looks down at her. He smiles and holds her jaw and you know she is protected.

Truth is, you envy Tom the ability to settle down. Is he not terrified of being wrong again? Discovering he's the defective one? He must think it was all you. One day you lost your mind. You woke up curled on the kitchen floor with nothing inside but a ball of twine to tie you to others. You had lost your mind, your bearings, yourself. Or maybe you never had them. But you couldn't find them with him. He was too big. Charismatic, like a Hollywood heartthrob or a dictator, depending on the weather. Are you with him or against him? Him and his assured dreams. Your wispy, ungrounded desires were no match. He had swallowed you and the only escape was to cut him open. Now you stick to small men with small mouths.

She invited you. You know it was her idea. And it makes you feel so insignificant. A benign cyst. You take comfort in reverse psychology. She invited you so you would think she thinks you're harmless, because in fact you're the furthest from it. What is her opinion of you? What picture has Tom painted? Why should you care? You're fucking a twenty-two-year-old. You should've brought him. She could see how far beyond Tom you've grown. You're the winner.

A gaggle of Sunny's clown-faced friends herd the crowd with exaggerated circling arms toward a corral of tents for the reception. Tables clothed in stomach-acid pink, places set with named chocolates. No rhymes. No *Together now but not sure how long: Sunny and Tom*. No *Together forever, really, it ain't funny: Tom and Sunny*. Yours holds your maiden name, which you do not go by. You are seated not at the cool-singles table, which holds the barber, the barista, the candlestick-maker, but at the pathetic, perma-singles table. Grey-rooted redheads and wild-bearded men wearing ties encrusted with soup from the last wedding they attended.

After the final bite of your vegan, gluten-free meal which you know she ordered from the caterer in order to seem like a martyr—you would've been fine with plain rice—Sunny sits between you and her cousin Jim from London. Ontario, not England, hahaha. She says, I'm so glad you came, and squints in a way you can't quite read. Fear? You want to offer a shoulder to cry on when times get tough. You know how he can be, you'll say, and to the confused scrunch of her features you'll raise your eyebrows and say, Oh, and watch her cheeks drop.

But you don't want to be that person. You've been reading books with *path* in the title. You're supposed to love everyone. Give without receiving. Equanimity. Happiness in others' accomplishments. Good for you, Tom. You found a desperate simpleton who has no style but only because she exerts her energy into being a good person. No. Good for you, Tom. You found someone empty enough to receive your overwhelming love. No. Someone open enough to receive it.

Thanks for inviting me, you say.

Of course, she says. It felt right.

So you're here for closure. You are a symbol, an object of the rejected, what they are moving past on their path.

It was almost as good as our wedding, you say, and immediately regret it. Sunny stares at the table, what else could she do? You clear your throat. But, you know. Bad wedding, good marriage.

How to stop yourself? Is it possible to speak with her as any other human? No, it is not. This is not a human you would ever speak with in any other circumstance. Ever. Not of your breed, your ilk. Equanimity, Meg. Equanimity. What can you say? *I can tell you make him happy.* Too superior. *Better luck this time.* No, obviously. All you can say is, I love your dress. This pleases her. She explains the dress-buying process down to the Latvian tailor who almost mixed up her bust and waist sizes—Can you imagine? A twenty-four bust and a thirty-six waist—and asks about yours.

I wore my grandmother's, you say. I was going to have my tailor cut neck and arm holes out of a white pillowcase, but I wore my grandmother's dress.

Maybe I should be quirkier, Sunny says.

Tom likes things simple.

Sunny slouches, which, in that dress, makes her décolletage wrinkle up like an uncertain pug. There are some people you can't have a conversation with.

It takes the sight of Sunny dancing with Sebastian—her arms around your son, *your* son—to propel you to Tom. You tap his shoulder. "Stairway to Heaven." Last dance.

Surprised you came, he says.

He dances like a twelve-year-old, his eight fingertips to your shoulders.

You pinch the pockets of his jacket and say, You put on a good wedding. You wait for him to reference your wedding, any sign you're still there, somewhere, but he does not. Equanimity, Meg. This isn't your day.

This was harder than I thought, you say. There are so many things you want to say. This could be the last time you hold his attention. I'm sorry for turning my back to you so many nights in bed. I'm sorry we created a life we couldn't protect. I'm sorry I grew up without you. What you do say is, Forgive me. He looks down at you. He smiles but does not hold your jaw.

The Rest of Him

Hair work-slicked and tie sagging, Nik lifts my covers and pokes me with a corner of envelope. From your mom, he says. He thanks me, with a generous helping of sarcasm, for ensuring our daughter got off to school on time, then informs me he has floor hockey with the boys tonight and I should not wait up. What grown man plays floor hockey?

Of course, after being incommunicado for over fourteen years, Mom sends me a newspaper article about Dad's severed foot. No note, no marginalia, not even penned devil's horns on his image. He's been dead to her for years, no need for fanfare.

I decide to leave the house with my mail and no plans to return. We'll see who shouldn't wait up for whom. My daughter's fourteen now—as long as she's got a buzzing rectangle of light in her palms, she doesn't care if I'm here or there. Nik's going through his sad-man phase and is no help at all. Sears went under four years ago and he hasn't worked since. He's not fancy enough for the Bay, too proud for Walmart. The only thing he's ever done is manage the men's department. His only skill is loyalty and I'm even less qualified. Now we live off EI and his mother's pity. We haven't told our daughter and Nik doesn't intend to. Every morning, he dresses for work and we slump off to hide out in separate coffee shops. I buy almond lattes in white mugs from a Scandinavian-looking couple with clear eyes and unclenched jaws. Nik buys Americanos in paper cups from young, dark-haired women with tattooed heads and effusive problems. I'll walk by his café of choice, saddled with legumes and leafy greens, and see him through the window, elbows to counter, body curled toward a shady pixie, nodding gracefully like he used to for me. It's easier to listen to troubles you can walk away from.

In Little Norway, the curly-haired wife delivers my almond latte and a cup of sparkling water and toast and jam for Jenny across the table. The wife has freckled, doughy cheeks and is bra-less under a black-and-white striped European boat shirt. How could anyone stray from a woman with cheeks like that?

Jenny's all *mmmph shoo good* with the jam. It's homemade, you know, she says.

I nod and pop bubbles in my water with my fingertip.

Jenny licks a bright red glob off her palm and tells me she thinks she's dating a married man.

You think he's married or you think you're dating?

Both.

Does he wear a ring?

Jenny nods, but gives me jazz hands. It could be decorative.

On his ring finger?

It's big and twisty. Not a band.

Have you kissed?

Jenny taps her cheek and presses her tongue into it.

Beej?

She flicks crumbs at me. He kissed me on the cheek.

I wouldn't want Nik doing that.

Men will be assholes.

You want to date an asshole?

If you cut out the assholes, what's left?

Flaccid, too-nice guys.

Jenny gags into my water glass. Right? she says. Khaki pants, duck-footed walk.

European man-bag.

Feathered hair.

Smiles at children in restaurants.

Those are the closet Paul Bernardos.

Are you seeing him tonight?

Jenny shrugs. He's kind of spur-of-the-moment.

Mind if I stay with you?

Jenny raises her eyebrows.

My dad died.

You have parents?

My mom mailed me this article.

I uncrumple the clipping. There's Dad onstage, hands groping a mic as though it was a cliff edge he was falling from.

Jenny's in her glazy-eyed new-man world and doesn't notice the headline. All she says is, Your dad's cute.

I read the headline: *Local Punk Pioneer Leaves Podiatric Puzzle*. Some hiker found my dad's foot on the beach.

Where's the rest of him?

Feet disarticulate from the body as a result of prolonged immersion in water, I read. *Separation is a natural element of the process of decomposition.*

He's decomposed?

He might not actually be dead.

Like a zombie?

Like Elvis.

Wouldn't Elvis be like a hundred? Jenny steals a sip of my latte and I can tell she wants to return to her agenda. She stares out the window and taps an appropriate twenty seconds with her finger on the table before asking, But if my guy is single, why would he wear any ring on his ring finger?

Maybe all his other fingers are too fat.

You think I shouldn't see him?

What would you get out of it?

Sex.

Vibrator?

The smell of a man.

Hard to replicate.

The smell of an asshole.

Do assholes smell better than nice guys? I look behind my shoulder to make sure the Scandinavian-looking couple isn't within earshot, on account of all the swearing and sexy talk and them being all white and sweet-tidy-clean, Belle-and-Sebastian-listening boppity-boop.

You went straight from the cradle to Nik, eh?

I had sex with the first guy I kissed in middle school. Ewen Moss. We were playing seven minutes in heaven. Had an abortion. After that I stopped shaving my pits and showering. Then I came to Edmonton and met Nik.

Damn, Sara. The seven minutes weren't for intercourse.

When were we supposed to say no?

You were supposed to let him unzip your jeans and get maybe three fingers in and then giggle all high-pitched until he stopped. You had no girlfriends?

There was this girl Rita. She had an overbite like Freddie Mercury but not his bone structure. Or stage presence. No guy would go near her.

Jenny picks up her plate and licks the crumbs off it.

I bet you had lots of friends, I say.

Nope. I was the mysterious slutty chick with a thirty-year-old boyfriend.

I was the mysterious slutty chick who'd only had sex once.

Those high school boys were so afraid of us.

I give Jenny a high five and ask if she thinks Nik is a nice guy or an asshole.

Nice guy, of course. But not quite flaccid.

I nod. I can't tell Jenny about the baristas. It seems so stupid. The father of her child was fucking dish pigettes under her nose before she even went into labour. But at least he was honest about it. And Jenny's my girl. I want to tell her about how Nik wears skid-marked sweats to bed now and how when I'm in my sex panties and I bend down to pet the cat and look through the nook in my armpit, he's not spying my ass, he's checking his phone for hockey scores or craft beer reviews. About how, when we do make love and I take off my shirt, he lowers his eyes and hands to my hips to avoid addressing how even tits so small as mine could droop. And about how once I've had one hairy ball in my mouth after the other and I spread his legs farther and run the tip of my tongue down till I feel him taut and tangy, he clenches up and pushes my head away and says he's not sure he wiped properly. And I want to ask her what to do. What do you do when you meet this guy when you're eighteen who seems quirky and cool and wears mismatched socks and peels Bosc pears for you and marks you like a dog with his saliva and then he turns into this slick-haired, finger-gun shooting, small-talk spewer who reserves his dwindling stores of kindness for a bunch of coffee-slinging angels of darkness who are young enough to befriend his daughter and are only kind to him in return because they're paid to provide superior customer service? What do you do with a crumb-by-crumb betrayal you only notice once there's not enough good left to spread the jam on?

But Jenny's idea of commitment is using the same shade of lipstick until the tube runs out, and she has yet to accomplish that. She's holding her hands together in that namaste way, telling me how nice-guy Nik is. How he makes those killer chicken wings and not too spicy the way most men would. How he coaches my daughter's softball team and how he looks at me in the same way he looks at our daughter. Proud and admiring and kind of worried. And this makes me cry with my palms to my eyes and hunched over my latte. And Jenny says, Oh shit, your dad.

But I know it's so much bigger than that.

Why are you avoiding Nik?

I shake my head.

Jenny waits for something to come out of my mouth and then finally says, Okay. She reaches out and presses her key into my palm. She says, I gotta get to work. Stay at my place as long as you want. The kid's with his dad this week so you can walk around in your panties and stuff. Jenny turns to leave then lunges back. That's my only key, so wear it around your neck.

When Jenny walks away she pulls my life force with her like a tide. I should have a reason to walk briskly from point A to B like she does, like all the people outside do, but I bet they all had fathers. Fathers who taught them to change a tire and growled at their boyfriends and gave them away to their husbands named Brad who are child psychologists or school principals and make them bulgur pilaf on Sundays and drive them to the lake in summer and otherwise bask with them in their normal, normal lives.

The Scandanavian-looking couple touch hips while one works the till and the other the espresso machine. The wife lets the husband go on about ideal brew time and doesn't roll her eyes when he dumps an espresso because it took thirty-one seconds to pull rather than the desired twenty to thirty. She doesn't joke that it's better too long than premature. Perhaps I've not chosen the most fitting coffee shop to patronize after all.

It's Monday, which means it's Margarita Monday at Julio's Barrio, and I am to meet Jenny here after work. I hope she won't show up with Some Of The Girls: her fellow office assistants with last-name first names like Mackenzie and Argyle who nibble at plain corn chips like field mice and don't order guacamole but eye me desperately and mumble dieting mantras while I eat mine. They drink tequila straight up because it has fewer calories that way and, after half an hour's passed, holler about Mike from accounting's tight pants and that time Kennedy ass-fucked Paul from marketing with a green highlighter, mistakenly using Elmer's rubber cement as lube, at the Legendary Office Christmas Party of 2019.

I'm under the Trump piñata, which is the most coveted seat in the joint. When a jumbo plate of nachos is ordered on Margarita Monday, the cooks play the Mexican hat dance and everyone bashes at Trump with replicas of fence posts from the Donald Trump Great Great Huge Wall of Mexico™ for the duration of the song. If there's a breach in the papier mâché, Donald spews gold-foiled chocolate coins, Cherry Bombers, canisters of orange spray-tan, fake "nacho-grade" tear gas, Nancy Pelosi action figures, faux squirrel skins and pink toques for all.

The last time I saw Trump burst was at Nik's fortieth birthday party five months ago. I jabbed the bat between Donald's eyes and tore him down to his bullfrog chin. Nik tipped his head to the ceiling and I popped Cherry Bombers down his throat. Nik held me with all his fingers entwined around my waist, exposed his cherry-red teeth and said, You are vicious and sublime. I told him he looked like a happy cannibal grabbing me so with his blood-red mouth. Any other time I would've bitten my tongue. He would've made some remark about a man's necessity for flesh and was there no respite from the vegan police with me around. But that night he tightened his grip and bit my neck. He took me home and fucked me like every inch of my body was a welcome surprise, like my every unconventionality was beautiful simply because it was mine. Then we woke up and he was forty. And he was not Don Draper or Jason Seaver or even George Jetson. He pierced his failings with metal hooks and hung them from my limbs and I became weighted and precarious with his discontent.

Jenny won't be here for another hour and my only entertainment is a window to Whyte Avenue. There's a girl with turquoise hair outside. It's short and juts from her scalp in felted clusters. She's painted her eyes glimmery peach all around. It brings out the red in her eyeballs, makes her look like a lab bunny—but in a good way. She's with this guy who has a kempt beard and wears a dark toque and coveralls ironically. Honestly, show me a clean-shaven man without a lid and I'll cream my panties. His jaw waggles and he slices the air between them, fingers stitched together like patronizing soldiers as he mansplains Tarkovsky's use of recurrent imagery, or perhaps why he believes her DivaCup is more harmful to the environment than tampons. That annoying voice in my head asks why I assume all men are dicks. Maybe he's pinpointing his areas of vulnerability with those shark-fin fingers.

I'm on my third margarita and Donald's looking more and more like a constipated orangutan swaying above my head when Jenny's giggle wafts in. She's accompanied by a pantsuited posse clicking toward me in five-inch heels. Argyle, Quinn, Emerson and some dude. They're all huddled, faces in, sweeping the bar like a tornado. I duck and run, tell the host they'll cover my bill, and escape out the back door. Quinn is the youngest office assistant at Jenny's work, fresh out of secretary school—an institution I thought had died with second-wave feminism. She's always touching my clothes and telling me how retro I look. Last time Jenny brought her out, Quinn told me she hopes she looks as good as me when she's old.

It's November freezing outside. Head-in-the-refrigerator cold. Not the best day to leave the house for good in a jean jacket and macramé scarf. The Edmontonians are huddled into their collars like frigid turtles, unaware of one another, not yet over October's on-again, off-again above-zero seductions, holding out for one more hit before December. I look for Nik's slick of black hair tucked into a pilling green wool overcoat, the slowly unravelling scarf I knitted but never finished for him on the seventh anniversary of my landing on his doorstep. The seventh is wool. He's not on the street. He's not inside his coffee shop. I press my face into the glass and wish for his presence. *My dad died*, I want to yell at him, *and here you are*. I want him to be as awful as I imagine him to be. To live up to my fear he won't return home at the end of each day. Because the alternative, the stripping off layers of yourself and feeding them to another like slices of prosciutto, feels infinitely more dangerous than solitude.

My tiny bladder leads me to tug at the coffee shop's door but they're closed for the night and the little Groke mopping the floor inside only shrugs at me. At Jenny's place, I pee and try a few of her prescription drugs. I spend far too much time searching for her son's diary. He's normally home when I visit—a greasy toad crumpled into his gaming remote on Jenny's plaid vintage recliner. Jenny uses the word *vintage* to describe anything she's found on the side of the road. How could I not take this opportunity to venture into his bedroom? This room's brand of funk is a mixture of rancid butter, rotten eggs and cloves. Cloves? No, mould.

There is no diary to be found, but atop a pile of dirty track pants is a captain's log–style notebook that deciphers butt days from abs days. He must be like Nik, with a little man inside his head who remembers everything perfectly as it happened, including every feeling he did not feel. Under Jenny's son's mattress next to the obligatory crusty sock is a stash of *Hustler* mags from the seventies he must've inherited from his on-again, off-again father. I haven't passed anything down to my daughter other than the mole under my left armpit, and neither of us knows what to do with that. We exist on different planets. If only we could gawk at a nice set of jugs and make magazines sticky together. What if she thinks of me the way I thought of my mother? What if my mother thought of me the way I think of my daughter? I take the *Hustler*s to the bathroom, run a bath and mix in all of Jenny's bubble flavours, from Sugar Plum Fairy to Grandma's Rose Garden. I spend quite some time practising the *Hustler* ladies' frog-legged, archy-backed, under the nipple boob-cupping, jaw-dropped, bottom half of two front teeth exposed poses in the bathroom mirror. I trim my pubes accordingly with Jenny's bang scissors. I lie in the bath, make bubble arm rests and pretend I'm Dr. Claw. I make bubble clouds and play Care Bears with Jenny's scrappy bits of soap. I lie very still and soak up all the hot until it's gone then add more and repeat. It's been so long since I've become pruney in the bath.

When I hear Jenny's drunken soft-whispered drawl and a low voice enter the apartment, the most important thing to take care of before I'm discovered seems to be wiping my stray hairs off her scissors, the bathroom floor, the toilet seat. Jenny puts on her Beach House playlist which means she's in for some serious panties-on couch action. If it was a panties-off night, she'd go for something less morose-'n'-dreamy and more sexy-fun, like a few of Grimes' higher pitched, breathy numbers on repeat. I think I'll be safe here in the bathroom, corpse-like in the tub, until Jenny and dude finish pressing hard parts against soft parts and grabbing at the bits of each other's bare skin that become exposed during said pressing. Until he says, I should go, and she says, Yeah, you should, and then bites his bottom lip one more time and he says, Jeeee-nny, in that you-naughty-naughty-girl voice.

We always think we're safe, don't we, until somebody needs to pee.

Jenny stumbles into the bathroom, twirls against the toilet, grabs the tub edge then makes eye contact with me through the foam. Jesus, Sara, she says, then she covers her mouth and spurt-laughs into her hand. She takes off her bra and panties, which was all she had on, and climbs in with me.

What about the dude? I whisper.

He can wait.

Is it the married guy?

Jenny nods.

Is he married?

Jenny nods and adds, But unhappily.

Who isn't?

Jenny holds my jaw with both of her hands and stares into my eyes. Are you okay?

I took some pills. I hold Jenny's wrists and say, I'm so good.

My antibiotics? You're hilarious.

I press my face into her chest, but the top part, so my chin rests on her boob. Men must like women who have actual boobs, I say.

I love your little bee stings. Jenny rubs a thumb over one of my nipples. I part my lips into her skin. It tastes like buttered flowers. Would it be so difficult for Nik to moisturize?

Didn't you need to pee? I say.

Already did.

I thought it got warmer.

Why'd you run out of the bar?

I don't know. Your work friends.

Jenny's hand is on my waist now, and she squeezes me like she's ripping apart a baguette. He won't fuck me, she says.

The wife?

If his penis doesn't cheat, he doesn't cheat.

I slide into Jenny and wrap my legs around her waist easy and slippy under the water. She licks my throat and I grab her ribs, each finger finds a little gap to fit into. I tilt my pelvis into her. Jenny grabs my bum and pulls me close. I bite her neck and cup one of her boobs. It feels weird to hold a boob from this side of things. Jenny runs two fingers between my bum cheeks. I press myself in and away from her soft belly and suck and suck at her neck. She mewls like a kitten, but a bit too loud. Is she here to score girl-on-girl sexy points with Married Dude?

Jenny? Is someone there? he says, and I hear the squeak of the vintage recliner.

All good, she yells. Be right out.

We should be together, I say.

We'd drive each other crazy.

I guess. You're so self-centred.

You're so high maintenance.

I curl my back away from Jenny and wrap myself into a ball. Really?

You think everyone's out to hurt you.

Everyone does hurt me.

You get too close. Jenny rests her elbow on the tub edge and laces her fingers together. You feel betrayed if I change my hair without you.

That one time, I say. I wanted pink hair too.

I take a deep breath and blow a canyon into my bubbles. I tell Jenny I thought my dad would come back and save me some day. But this is my life.

Maybe he only lost a foot at sea. Maybe he's a pirate.

He used to call me Jellybean. The day he left, he called me Sara. I should've stopped him.

He would've left some other day.

Nik hasn't spoken my name in months.

He would've left by now.

He has these baristas.

At least he's not... Jenny wags her thumb toward the bathroom door. He probably thinks I'm massively constipated.

Blame your period.

Jenny wraps herself in a towel and goes out like that, leaving her bra and panties like snotty tissues under a sick bed. I hear her say good night to Married Dude. I hear her say she likes spending time with him and I hear him say, This was fun. I hear him tell her she's cute and sexy, but he never says beautiful. I hear him tell her to take good care and to keep in touch and then I hear Jenny's door close. I hear Jenny repeat, slow and soft, Keep. In. Touch. I leave the bathroom wrapped in a towel of my own. I lean into her from the back, skin to skin, terry to terry. I rest my lips on her shoulder and hold her hand.

Jenny and I sleep in her bed with our underwear on. She twists around me and falls asleep squeezing me like I don't require oxygen. Nik in bed behind me is long and lean and elastic, like a whisk. I miss his fingers between my thighs and the smell of his bedtime breath. Toothpaste mint overcome by summer-lawn mouth. I will return home for breakfast tomorrow. I'll sit between my daughter and Nik at the kitchen table. My daughter will say, Where'd you come from? and Nik will put a bagel in the toaster for me without asking where I was, without saying anything. I'll wait for the right time to tell him about my dad, like during a commercial break when the Oilers have just scored, as Nik rides their momentum, able to morph elation into sympathy. He'll look into my eyes and tell me he's sorry. And not only for the loss of my dad. Nik will be sorry for every time I've lost him—to his insular worries, to his misplaced ambition, to all the twenty-five-year-old girls he's wanted to absorb his shame. I'll look him back in the eye and I'll thank him. And I will be thankful for his sympathy and his remorse, but most of all for the few seconds he waits once the Oilers are back on the ice before reverting his eyes to the TV.

After Gwen

Shepps obeyed Gwen when she told him to go away. He roared away in his Westfalia and spent his nights warming the Crystal Pool's parking lot with his exhaust, his mornings warming its public toilets with his feces. Every part of him ached for Gwen. Every synapse in his brain was a GWEN receptor, every blood cell was not white or red but Gwen, every sperm was programmed to swim to Gwen. Days he worked at the Esso, he spelled her name in M&Ms on the counter and nibbled her away, or he inhaled diesel fumes and imagined her vapourizing out of gas tanks in technicolour mist. At night, he lay in his Westie's loft bed with one hand around the neck of his bass guitar, the other hand slathered in petroleum jelly, his mind on Gwen. She wore different heads. At times her own, at times Shepps' kindergarten teacher's, and at times she wore Damian Costello's. Her body was as Shepps recalled. Back arched, her nipples like red rolling pin handles pointed to the sky and her mouth gaped—a cavernous, fiery entrance to hell.

After a couple of months, Gwen's back began to hunch, her nipples shrunken and dangling like burnt-out Christmas lights.

Her face became a swirl of features, none of them hers. His kindergarten teacher's muddy St. Bernard eyes, Damian's thin-lipped smirk. One evening after leaving the Esso, Shepps drove up to Gwen's building and parked under her bedroom window. He hoped for a glimpse of her undressing to rebuild his mental inventory. A recollection of a shadow of underarm hair, the curve and heft of a bum cheek, the nub of a baby toe, even. His stomach clenched for fear she'd see him. His stomach clenched tighter for fear he'd see her with another man—some wiry punk with sunken features, long graceful fingers and a sleek penis—someone nothing like Shepps, with his broad shoulders desirous of more muscle than he had to give, his pepperoni stick fingers that fumbled for her clit, the pendulum cock whose girth he apologized for every time she screamed.

Gwen appeared on her balcony within seconds, as though she had spent the days since his departure creeping about, shushing her young daughters, listening for his *put-put-put*.

She rested an elbow on the rail and said, I thought I told you to go away.

Shepps leaned out of his passenger side window. You didn't tell me to stay away.

Ten minutes later, framed by the open sliding door of his van, a tuft of cardboard-brown hair, tail-light nipples under a shredded tee and a hint of saggy, greying panty crotch.

You were fading, Shepps said. He squatted on the van floor in front of her.

Gwen raised her fingers to Shepps' cheeks and tucked them, through his stubble, into the line of his jaw. Don't you want to forget me? she said. She leaned into him and sucked on his bottom lip.

Shepps shook his head no.

Gwen kissed him. She licked his teeth, tickled the roof of his mouth with her tongue. But I'm so awful, she said.

Shepps shook his head again. You're so lovely.

He grabbed Gwen under her armpits, lifted her into the van and up to the loft. He held her ribs and pressed the side of his face into her. Her erratic heart a lazy woodpecker at his ear. This was how new parents must feel, this fanatic love for the unknown.

Close the fucking door, she said. I'm in my panties.

Shepps slid the door closed. Gwen relaxed into his hands and he squeezed and pulled and sucked at her, supple and salty as play clay. Gwen came as Shepps had hoped. She arched her back, hands to her heels and cawed like a seagull on garbage day. Then she uncorked Shepps' cock and turned to face the windshield.

My kids are upstairs, she said. She dangled her legs off the loft and dusted sand from between her toes. You ever vacuum this thing?

How would I?

Dustbuster?

Can you stay a little longer?

The girls are alone. It's illegal, I think.

I could come up.

I don't want to confuse them. They've already said goodbye.

What if I stay? For good.

We tried that.

Shepps lifted himself to his elbows. We could try again, he said. Really try.

I did really try, Gwen said.

She hopped down from the bed and picked her panties like a blackberry from a nook of Shepps' van. See you next time you're lonely, she said. She stepped out of the van and wiggled her fingers at him.

I'm always lonely.

Gwen didn't turn around. She cackled and scuffed her bare feet along the sidewalk and into her apartment building.

Every night for the following weeks, Shepps found himself under Gwen's bedroom window, under the spell of her Bat-Signal nightlight, under her. The nights began with her soft in his hands and ended with her rigid-backed cry to the roof, her trundle back inside. As the weeks wore on, it became easier to watch Gwen walk away. When she returned, there was a little less of her. She became less pliable, her scream a muted squawk. She would not let him into her home, her life. They had nothing to talk about, no knowledge of the other's days. Shepps wallpapered his heart with thinning layers of Gwen.

One night, as Gwen shuffled back to her building, Shepps yelled after her, You didn't even say hello.

Gwen turned. Hello, she said. Goodbye.

Is that it?

See you tomorrow, she said.

I don't think you will. Shepps stepped out of his van, toward Gwen.

You busy?

No, he said. I don't—

Stop. Gwen held her two middle fingers up and backed into her building. Go away, she said. Stay away.

Shepps knew he would regret leaving Gwen—forever this time. She was a cancer, a tsunami, a nuclear disaster. A force so powerful she had divided his life into before and after. He squeezed his eyes shut to stamp into his memory this brand of emptiness. Not after-Gwen emptiness, full of longing, but during-Gwen emptiness, in which she stole his longing and replaced it with nothing but a familiar body.

November trees stretched flaming arms against a charcoal sky. The time of year Victoria-based van dwellers regretted their housing decisions. Shepps enacted life coated in a moist film. At the Esso, with nobody's name to diligently spell out, he poured bags of M&Ms down his throat. He inhaled diesel fumes and imagined nothing save for the odd large-breasted dragon. At night, he gave up masturbation altogether. This was non-Gwen emptiness. Truly empty emptiness.

Until Shepps played his bass. He hadn't touched it—musically—since his band's last gig almost a year earlier, December 13, 1990. They opened D.O.A.'s farewell show at the Commodore in Vancouver. D.O.A. got back together soon after. It was Shepps' band that said farewell for good. Damian walked away from everyone after that show—the band, Gwen, his daughters. No one had seen him since. There were rumours he was playing a weekly gig at a country bar in Banff, or that he'd joined the crew of a pirate ship. Last Shepps heard, Donny moved to Olympia to play with Fitz of Depression. Ricky stuck around Victoria tending to his pot plants and working construction. He'd kept a good beat but his heart was never in it. Shepps was the only willing member left.

He spent those damp, Gwen-less nights composing songs to the quick slapping of his D-string. Wretched love songs, songs about M&Ms, songs about coins found between van cushions. He took the stage once a week at an open mic in a divey tea house in James Bay decorated with jars of pickled eggs and doilies. He developed a fan base. Mostly retired lawyers having a second crack at their teenaged Neil Young fantasies. But there was a girl. Magda. She played acoustic guitar and sang about *Degrassi High* plotlines, Jesus and swing sets. A warm, bubble-gum pink cloud surrounded her. She smiled and clapped her hands (off-time and inappropriately, given the morose content) while Shepps played. She wore push-up bras and dressed in pastels. Her socks matched the colour of her shirts. Her hair was so shiny he wondered if it was synthetic, like that of the My Little Ponies he'd spent hours brushing for Gwen's daughters.

One night, she sang of heartache. A boy had left, left, left her at the movies with her tick, tick, ticket in hand. She drank tears, tears, tears and soda and cough, cough, coughed on her popcorn. When she curtsied and sat back down, Shepps sidled up to her table.

True story?

Magda turned the shade of a plum blossom. She nodded.

Choke might work better.

Pardon?

Choke, choke, choked on my popcorn?

You're good at that.

Shepps ran a stilted hand through his shaggy dark curls. You wanna check out my van?

Magda was pretty and simple and easy. Her belly button was a taut mini Timbit, not a sleepy hungover eyelid like Gwen's. She was a virgin and only dallied above the belt but she nodded encouragingly, fluffy towel at the ready, while Shepps masturbated with her legs wrapped around his waist. On hot nights, she let Shepps suck at her nipples and dropped her hand on top of his hand. She petted his twitching fist and called him *baby* which, what with the nipple sucking, was disconcerting but sweet. A pleasant, hand-held stroll toward an orgasm, not an unrestrained black bear's growl of a release.

Magda had twenty years to Shepps' thirty and lived in a bungalow near Hillside Mall with her devoutly Christian parents. They did not believe in premarital dating and spent much of their time sifting through a selection of appropriately God-fearing and employed suitors their daughter would reject, insisting she'd rather care for her parents than a stranger. Meanwhile, Shepps was granted residency on their driveway as a lost soul Magda met while street proselytizing. He was not allowed access to their home, but Magda snuck into his van most nights with leftovers and clean laundry. When Magda and her parents left for prayer group, Shepps slithered through an open kitchen window and partook of their hot water and antibacterial products.

Shepps and Magda formed a duo. Shepps aimed for a Thurston and Kim vibe but they landed closer to Ian and Sylvia. They called themselves Jesus's Beard, which Shepps found funny and Magda found reverent. They combined their repertoires and played discordant tunes about Jesus finding quarters in swing sets made of M&Ms and pregnant, suicidal teenagers holding hands in the back seats of vans. They were the stars of the tea house stage. It gave the regulars hope to see something productive come of the open mic.

Magda was perfect. Textbook perfect. Romantic-comedy perfect. If only Shepps could live and die by her moods, the smell of her funk or the heat of her breath against his skin. But Magda was even-tempered, smelled like magazine perfume inserts, and her body temperature never exceeded warm. When Shepps asked her for songwriting topics, she said, I don't know. When he changed a chord, she said, Sure. Shepps was suffocating in Magda's pink cloud of compliance. He was a giver, a follower. He absorbed the personalities of others and reflected them back in the most pleasing light. He was the tofu. When Magda would look to him, wide-eyed, for direction, he tightened. Shepps was not tight. Shepps was a flailing windsock in a hurricane, twisting wildly toward anyone who would take him in. Shepps was accustomed to rejection, indifference, mockery.

He attempted to scrape through Magda's mist to her truth. Her opinions, her passions, her anger. He wanted to scorch his hands on her magmatic core. He made empty promises to bring home Hershey's Kisses from the Esso. He changed their duo's name to the Shepps Project. He spilled ketchup and black tea on her mother's favourite church blouse. He forgot Valentine's day. To all of this Magda said only, *To err is human* and, *Okay*.

And then Shepps saw Gwen. His van had been monogamously parked in Magda's driveway for months. He'd barely thought of Gwen. Two or three times a day at most. Gwen was leaning against the glass of a dollar store downtown, her eldest tugging her toward the bags of marbles inside, her youngest wrapped around her bare leg. Gwen was dressed for winter on top—flannel lumberjack shirt, toque, mitts—but jean cut-offs and flip-flops on bottom. Her thighs were heroin-thin. When Shepps called her name, she startled, and held a protective arm out in front of her girls.

Oh, she said. You.

Hey Gwen. Hi girls.

The girls looked at Shepps, then back to the marbles behind the glass.

Your van here? Gwen said. I need to get home.

Sure, yeah. Shepps pointed up the street.

Gwen shuffled into the van behind the girls, catatonic, weighted by a clinking backpack.

Where you parking these days? she said as they climbed up Fort.

My girlfriend's.

You haven't been around.

We have a band.

I met someone in a band too. He's… Steve. He's away now's why I need a ride.

Sounds nice. I'm glad.

You should be.

I am.

Shepps stopped at Gwen's building and rummaged through his cupboards to find a few apples, half a loaf of bread, a brick of cheese. He displayed these to her and filled the empty spaces in her backpack, those not occupied by vodka bottles, while she crawled into the back to unbuckle her girls. In case Steve's gone a while, he said.

I don't need your charity, she said. She zipped up her bag, though, and took it, tumbling out of the van after her girls. She paused in front of Shepps' sliding door, girls aligned close like ducklings. She leaned into the door frame, her lips quivering.

Is she better than me?

Yes, he said.

Gwen nodded, waited for more. But Shepps said good-bye. He slid the door closed on Gwen's single-mom *American Gothic*—backpack for a pitchfork, egg-eyed girls for a wife—and he drove away.

What did Gwen expect? Is Magda better than you? Yes. Anyone is. If you strip Magda of her layers all you'll find is light. If you push her, you know which way she'll fall. She eats doughnuts with a spoon. Her body is perfectly hairless. Yes, she's better. But she's not you, she's not you, she's not you.

That night, Magda entered Shepps' van with a half-empty pan of mac and cheese resting on her forearms and a bag of chocolate chip cookies tucked under an armpit, but Shepps had lost his appetite. All he could think about was Steve. Steve, who was ninety-nine percent certainly made up. Though he could exist. He could fill Gwen's cupboards with Kraft Dinner and vodka, he could ensure her daughters brushed their teeth before bed and left the house in pants, he could rip clumps of Gwen's hair when she demanded it, then hold her ear to the soft place under his collarbone all night. And if he did, where would that leave Shepps? Shepps wanted to be the put-upon martyr, the abused. He wanted to stew without Magda's unclouded eyes on him. The invisibility of the lesser.

Should we practise tonight? Magda said.

Shepps perforated the muculent heap of noodles with his fork.

Open mic is tomorrow, she said.

Maybe you should go solo.

Magda closed her lips around one slimy macaroni noodle, chewed ten times without separating her lips, swallowed. Did she ever drool? Slurp, burp, fart? Did her body even produce saliva?

If that's what you want, she said.

What do you want?

I want you to be happy.

You're so goddamned nice to me.

I love you.

That's not love, Shepps said.

Magda's jaw unhinged.

Shepps stopped himself from going further, from telling Magda she was parasitically thriving on filling his needs. He'd been there before, but this time he was the Gwen. You were better solo, he said. That movie song was really good.

Magda squeezed her fingers around her fork. I don't understand.

I have to go.

Single tears dropped from Magda's cheeks, as though choreographed to induce pity. Who are you? she said.

Exactly.

Gwen appeared like a poltergeist—finger-in-a-light-socket hair, wisp of a white nightdress, spread palms to his van window. She looked more radiant than when she brushed her hair, washed her face, accessorized. She crawled into Shepps' van and crouched against the sliding door.

I don't know why I came here, Shepps said.

Am I so awful?

I keep thinking I've reached my limit.

I don't deserve you. Gwen shed tears. Real, raccoon-eye tears. She twirled the strap of her nightie around an index finger.

I can barely leave the house. I need vodka to breathe. I need you.

Steve?

You, Shepps.

Gwen rarely humanized Shepps with a name. He sat cross-legged on the floor in front of her and held her hand.

I'm so afraid of everything outside my door. She propelled her face into his shoulder, streaked it with strokes of black mascara.

Let me come up, Shepps said. Take care of you.

Gwen climbed onto Shepps' lap. She put a fistful of nightie into his palm and licked his ear. Don't talk about us, she said. Let me stay here tonight.

And they repeated their sequence. Kiss, kiss, tongue, bite, kiss, earlobe, sweater, neck, neck, throat, bite, T-shirt, kiss, tongue, tongue, belt, kiss, kiss, bite, pants, fuck, fuck, fuck, fuck, come. Gwen lay naked beside him and sucked drops of sweat from his ribs. Life seemed pointless without her body next to his. He could either die then or lie there forever. He knew she would leave him. She might come back, repeat. The only thing he felt certain of was her eventual departure.

Is this what we are now? Shepps said.

Gwen rubbed her forehead into his armpit. What is this?

Come, go. Hot, cold.

Passion.

Can we fit in between?

What's in between? Stay. Warm. Stay warm.

Sounds nice.

Sounds like being stuck in the bath.

Will you ever let me up?

Gwen raised herself to her elbows. She looked into Shepps' eyes and slowly shook her head. You hate me more than you love me, she said.

Shepps left the city that morning with one last look at Gwen, curled behind her bedroom window, most likely searching for a pair of unsoiled underwear on the floor, tiny rolls of stomach supporting iv-bag breasts. Her obliviousness to the peeping eyes of the outside world so endearing. It's fine, she would say. Nobody looks up. Shepps drove up island until he was almost out of gas, to Buckley Bay, the ferry to Denman and then another to Hornby Island. It was almost June. Soon, the ice cream truck would pull up outside the Hornby Co-op, local girls would wander in flip-flops and string bikinis, tonguing toppling worlds of ice cream, their brown bums like fresh rolls steaming under cropped surf tees. Little Tribune Bay would be populated with naked middle-aged women, proudly or obliviously bushed, strolling through clear waters along the tide line, exuding a beauty richer than that of the spray-tanned, big-city weekend imports who ducked underwater and resurfaced nude, then squealed back to driftwood huts, breasts covered by forearms, their eyes full of the judgement borne by uncertainty.

Shepps parked his van at the Co-op campground all summer, which led to fall, and then to winter. Gwen existed in the swampy underlayer of his mind until forced to the surface by a woman at the Co-op with an unkempt nest of nearly dreaded sandstone brown hair, or by a set of large-nippled pancakes kissing the waves in Little Tribune. With these sightings came the if-onlys. If only she hadn't, if only she wasn't. If only her raw honesty, her morbidity, her confidence, her lips were superimposed onto somebody kind, compassionate, respectful. We could be so. He imagined conversations in which she listened, saw, agreed. Perhaps repented, begged. At times, she swirled downward into a cauldron of cartoonish green venom gushing from her dead, black heart.

He rode out the winter on Hornby performing odd jobs for widows—patching holes in water reservoirs, building chicken coops, pulling ivy, fennel and broom—and spent the summer fixing his van and singing to his bass lines at the Saturday market. He planted a garden beside the Co-op office. Carrots, tomatoes, kale, cannabis. He tended to his plants and they nourished him. This was the healthiest relationship Shepps had ever maintained. Lonely nights, he stroked the curves of his kale leaves. Tickled their serrated edges with the tips of his fingers. He kneeled in the wet loam and licked from stem to leaf tip, bit at and chewed their bitter tang.

—

The summer of '94, Shepps' third summer on Hornby, topics of discussion among tourists revolved around Kurt Cobain's suicide, planned trips to Seattle, Courtney Love murder conspiracy theories and coffee. The ice cream truck began to serve espresso. The girls at the beach dressed like their grandfathers—pleated tan pants slung low to their pubic bones, brown cardigans over bikini tops and knitted fingerless gloves. They all simmered in angst and pre-emptive grunge nostalgia. They mistrusted anyone who smiled.

Shepps' odes to kale didn't inspire the Saturday market crowd to part with their coins. He adopted a melancholic slouch, an anguished squint, directed his Afrotic curls to hang despondently like Eddie Vedder's and added "Something in the Way" to his repertoire. His between-songs banter included references to the van he lived in under a willow tree, which was Hornby Island's answer to a bridge. After his set one end-of-August Saturday, a pair of thin legs, bare save for a stripe of dark stubble the razor had missed, stood uncomfortably close. Gwen. Just when he'd stopped scanning crowds for her scuffy, pigeon-toed walk, when a female figure with two little girls in tow no longer took his breath. Gwen.

You've bought into that Seattle bullshit.

I'm a people pleaser.

I wondered where you took off to. I'm here with some guy. He has a cabin.

Sounds serious.

He's over by the mangoes with the girls. I noticed you and… I heard your voice, actually.

Good to see you, Gwen.

I've missed you.

Shepps collected the change from his guitar case and put it in his pocket. Enough to take Gwen and the girls for an ice cream and a coffee. Convince her to ditch Mango Guy. To turn passion and muted hatred into love, whatever that was. But having a taste of real Gwen would feed his fantasy, spike him from contentment to elation and then plummet him into misery when she walked away. He tidied his bass, folded up his chair and hoped Gwen would leave him numb and alone. Content.

Busy now? she said.

Sort of.

You like it here?

It's a good life.

Lonely?

Winter, a bit.

And summer?

Summer's busier.

You don't get tired of chasing girls?

Shepps snapped his guitar case closed. No girls, Gwen. Gardening, mostly.

So you're lonely.

Plants are reliable.

Gwen grabbed his hips and pressed her chest into his ribs. I'm lonely too, Shepps.

He kissed her hairline. It's lonely either way.

With me?

Yeah, he said. And her incomprehension made him feel lonelier still.

Shepps tucked his hands into his pockets. Shuffled the quarters and loonies around. He felt Gwen's hands on his sides, her curled fingers could either dig farther in or flick him away.

Gwen dropped her hands. You think Courtney killed him? Not at all.

Gwen nodded and spent some time kicking a hole in the dry dirt beside Shepps' guitar case. She reached out to him, touched his arm, but when Mango Guy beckoned from the quilt raffle stand, Gwen walked away.

Shepps did not see Gwen again for over twenty-five years. He stayed on Hornby and became a splash of colour on the island's palette. He learned some classic folk tunes on guitar. He was the soundtrack for country dances, golden anniversary parties and tourist weddings. He led a celibate existence save for the odd fresh divorcee or recurring tourist. He did not fall in love again. His apathetic heart belonged to his plants and to Gwen. He packaged her into his mind-murk as one indelible memory. The first day they met. Twenty-one years old, a waitress at Pluto's Diner, sticking a flyer for his band's show to the wall with her gum. She knew what came out of his mouth was a load of testosterone-pumped horseshit and she told him so. And when he left the diner that day having licked the sweat from her thighs, he felt addictively victorious. He'd spent every day since then willing anything other than Gwen to exist.

Shepps left Hornby Island after his fifty-fifth birthday, when he felt it wise to live on a bigger island, one with a hospital, one that might not be swallowed by the Pacific when the big earthquake hit. He ferried to Vancouver Island and parked his van back at the Crystal Pool in Victoria. He found a job at the public library shelving books—a job a teenager could do, a job teenagers *did* do. After a few years, he achieved Yoda status with his peers. They came to him for help with math homework, dispensary recommendations. He had veto power in squabbles over who had to tidy the children's area where parents divined meaning from iPhones while their children flung books and smashed keyboards.

Shepps was lured into a scandalous affair by Olivia, the children's librarian. Scandalous not due to its extramarital nature on her part, but to the hierarchical canyon between them—she being a step below the CEO and he being a step above janitorial. There was no courting period, no pursuit. One rainy lunch hour found them alone in the staff room, Shepps admiring the presentation of her salad. A bed of dark greens layered with julienned peppers, emaciated tomato circles and radish roses.

My husband, she said, cares very much how things look.

Shepps nodded and returned to his tuna casserole.

I hate him, Olivia said.

They ate in silence, Olivia's vitriol hanging between them and Shepps unable to think of what might properly diffuse it. Olivia destroyed the last of the radish roses with her molars. She cleaned between her teeth with a fingernail, then asked, You here 'til five?

Shepps nodded.

You drive a Westie, right?

Another nod.

Shall I join you after work?

Shepps nodded a final time. Not out of desire for her, but a desire to please, and to avoid the awkwardness of a rejection.

Olivia kept strict rules for Shepps. He was not to speak to her or even look at her at work. If he could glance like a normal person it would be fine, Olivia told him, but he could not help but ogle. She left him notes between books in various sections depending on her mood. On good days, she'd leave him naughty drawings and instructions to meet in the back corner of the local history room at noon inside the *Lesbian Sex Bible* 306.7663 CAG. Guilty days, she'd leave him a graphite-slathered torn sheet a few books down, inside *Collateral Damage: Guiding and Protecting your Child through the Minefield of Divorce* 306.89 CHI. Most days he'd find an apology and a goodbye housed between the pages of *The Breakup Bible* 155.643 SUS. On those days he'd lock himself in the single-stall bathroom and spend his lunch hour sobbing into salami on rye and projecting the details of his irritable bowel syndrome to the barrage of patrons who banged at the door. Olivia would catch up to him as he fumbled with his van keys at the end of the day and press her lips into the back of his neck. Forget the note, she'd say. I need you. He did not understand how this had happened, how he had come to care. Was he nothing but a dog responding to pleasure and pain? Weren't we all?

He knew this wasn't love—love was what he felt for Gwen. He had been drawn to Olivia by the masochism that first drew him to Gwen. But Gwen did more than spit at him as he knelt before her. She was history, tenderness made sweeter with doses of cruelty, she was need—not as a cog in her machine of retribution, but true need. To serve Gwen made him feel worthwhile, absolved of all the awful things he'd ever done and would ever do to any others.

While feeling through the 300s for a note one day, Shepps came across a young girl in the body of a woman. An unbrushed, unwashed bun of curls hovered over a stack of books topped with *Perfect Daughters: Adult Daughters of Alcoholics* 362.2923 ACK. She still smelled faintly of apricot jam and glue sticks.

Meg, he said.

She looked up and narrowed her eyes.

I'm Shepps. You probably don't remember me.

I've heard your name. She stood up, rested her book stack on her hip.

I used to... I lived with you and your mom and your sister for a bit.

I remember having some sort of father for a while.

How is your mom?

Not well, Meg said and pointed to her book stack.

I haven't seen her in years. She living in the same place?

Meg nodded, but slowly, with wary, slitted eyes.

You don't want me to?

Tough love, Meg said.

Shepps desperately wanted to see Gwen, to throw a rock at her window, even, and see what would happen. But tough love was not the kind of love Shepps gave. If Gwen opened her door to him, Shepps would wash her crusty, yellowed bedsheets. He would draw baths. He would spoon-feed her celebrity culinary couples: bacon and eggs, tea and honey, peanut butter and jam. All she'd have to do is hold his bottom lip between hers and ask if he would bring home a bottle of vodka to take the edge off, and he'd give in. He had to ignore now-Gwen in service of forever-Gwen.

After seeing Meg, Shepps wiped Olivia from his mind. There wasn't much difference during work hours, what with her rules. But one evening, at his van, Shepps felt the spine of a book hurled at the back of his neck. He turned to find Olivia shaking *Lolita* NAB at him in one hand and a note in the other. I left this for you a week ago, she said. She smacked the note into his cheek and walked away. *I saw you*, it said, in the thick, dark lettering of an intensely fisted pencil. And lower down, thick enough to rip through the paper: *pedophile*.

She's my girlfriend's daughter, he yelled after Olivia.

Olivia stopped. Whipped around and marched back toward Shepps. Girlfriend?

Ex-girlfriend.

You're cheating?

You're cheating, Shepps said.

Not on you.

Who do you go home to?

Olivia stared at Shepps, then threw her fists to the sky like a foiled villain. You're not who I thought you were, she screamed.

Shepps nodded. I'm not your spineless loser.

That night, Shepps walked to Gwen's building with his six-string strapped to his back. He sat under her window, close to the wall under her balcony so she couldn't see him, and he played for her. Lullabies, campfire songs, a lot of Joni Mitchell. He wanted her to know he was there, but unconsciously, in her dreams.

Shepps didn't knock on Gwen's door until two years later, on November 26, 2021. In his hand he clutched a newspaper article: *Local Punk Pioneer Leaves Podiatric Puzzle*.

Gwen stood in her doorway cradling a mug of tea in her palms. At fifty-nine, she looked almost the same as she did the last time he saw her. Her cheeks succumbed to a tired sag, her eyes floated the same purple tide. But she was fully dressed now, inconspicuous in jeans and a T-shirt. Pants zipped, armhole stitching intact, and was that a bra strap? He'd expected to find her naked in a fetal heap, clinging to a vodka bottle she'd grown around like moss. He'd half-expected to have to break down the door.

The last person I expected, she said.

I came because... Shepps held up the article.

Damian Costello, Gwen said airily. I thought he was invincible.

I always thought I might see him again.

Gwen dropped her head and nodded. She closed her eyes and palmed her cheeks. Shepps was her real love, but Damian was her mad love, the inaccessible one.

I don't know why I'm crying, she said. He's been dead to me for years. Ages.

Because it's Dams.

Shepps wiped the hair from her eyes. Gwen slapped Shepps' shoulder.

I'm finally divorced. She fell into his chest, scratched her head into his throat, held the back of his neck.

They stayed that way a while, slow dancing to the sound of their silent, unrhythmic sobs. When Shepps finally unbowed his head, Gwen lowered her hands from his body and walked to the kitchen. She made them tea in a clay pot, served on a wooden tray with matching vessels for cream and sugar. She placed it on the carpet at Shepps' feet and they sat on either side, cross-legged.

Cream in tea, Gwen said. My only vice.

There are worse things.

They filled the gaps in one another's histories, periodically interrupting with, *Little Meggie has a son?* Or, *In the local archives? Totally naked?* There was no jealousy, no yearning to have been there. Acceptance of the other's life as it had been lived. Appreciation of the other here, now.

When they both confessed they hadn't fallen in love again, Gwen said, Are our worlds too small?

Not at all, Shepps said. He reached across the tepid pot and held her hand in his palm, his fingers around her small wrist. He felt her pulse—not a beat frenetic with infatuation, but the ebb and flow of blood from her persistent heart.

Floating in the Maybe

Meg lifts her skirt. When her bare thighs hit the fine porcelain of Victoria's hippest cocktail bar, out sprays diarrhea like a blow from an orca. The woman in Blundstones in the stall beside her snorts. Meg will have to sit here until all who've witnessed her skirling anus have left the bathroom, the bar even, because by the time she emerges, there's no doubt everyone will have caught wind of the woman in bright-green Fluevog clogs who literally can't keep her shit together.

Sara waits for her at the bar on a cedar-wedge stool, dressed in black from T-shirt to Chuck Taylors, slurping at a Cheeky Gonzales like a sassy stagehand. Meg brought Sara to this bar on their way home from the airport to impress her with what Victoria has become in the nineteen years since she took off— look at these egg white–keen mixologists, large-goggled servers and denim-wedgied patrons; look at what we've accomplished without you.

Sara has returned to Victoria to celebrate their father's life. Three weeks ago, their mother texted a *Times Colonist* article to Meg about his disembodied foot. This is how she informed

Meg of her father's death. Since then, Meg has single-handedly summoned the shrapnel of his life—ship's crew, hairdressers and drummers who answered her ad in the *Georgia Straight*, the long-lost members of his punk band and Sara—in order to celebrate it. She's rented a hall, ordered daisies and poppies, blown up a grainy photo of her father at the point of his life she imagines her guests will want to celebrate—blond bull-kelp fronds of hair billowing across his face, tight jeans held up by his hooked low back, bird arms spastic and tangled in a mic cord.

Once the last Birkenstock shuffles out of the ladies' room, Meg tiptoes from her stall and to the mirror. She soaps her hands and holds them under warm water. She looks at herself. Not in the eyes, but in the chin, where her stress has accumulated in a constellation of pimples. She breathes in. *He didn't care.* She breathes out. *So why do you?* Meg looks herself in the eye now and repeats: He didn't care, so why do you?

Back at the bar, Meg hoists herself atop her stool, clogs dangling. Sara siphons her drink up her straw then tilts her head back and mama-birds it down her throat. They look at one another, pursing lips, inhaling in anticipation of an expansion of the small talk that expired in the cab on the way here, then exhaling, silent and defeated.

Ready for tomorrow? Meg said.

Do I need to do anything?

I've done it. Food, the band. Mom thought eulogies would be cheesy.

We're not allowed to talk?

Did you want to say something?

No. Didn't know I wasn't allowed, though.

Mom doesn't like hearing nice things about him.

Didn't know it was her night.

I don't want her to… maybe you could talk between sets.

Sara stabs at a lime wedge with her straw. Dorothy's Rainbow is playing?

Yeah, I got the band back together.

Like the Eagles.

God, I hope not.

Meg and Sara share their first laugh of the evening. Maybe ever. Meg clutches at her stomach, picturing a clump of withered old men buckled under the weight of their guitars, playing punk rock, of all things, at a funeral. She gasps for air, hopes she doesn't laugh out any more of the curdled contents of her intestines.

Meg's phone buzzes with a text from Mark, the inappropriately young gender studies classmate she invited as her plus-one to the celebration of life. His reply: *Sounds fun??? Can't make it.* Meg chastises herself for misinterpreting Mark's attention as Benjamin Braddock-esque flirtation rather than an attempt to score notes from the mature student who doesn't spend class time scrolling through her Instagram and who cluelessly wears skin-tight mom jeans when clearly mom jeans are only hot on non-moms who are scarcely old enough to bear children and who wear them ironically and not with the intent of covering, with a swath of stretch denim, the jellyfish of flesh that has clung to their abdomen since giving birth eight years ago.

Meg knows it's wrong to desperately want a date for her father's celebration of life. A distraction from every person in attendance who will have known her father better than she did. In the few weeks since his death, nothing has seemed conscious. All the voices in her head, even that of reason, have reverted to an id state. She started last week with Greg, her economics tutor, whom she welcomed on her loveseat, bare legs butterflied around an open bottle of Malbec, childish breasts loose under an old lover's itchy sweater vest. Before he even reached for his notebook, sandwiched between D&D monster manuals in his backpack, Meg pushed Greg down by the shoulders until he crouched, salmon sweatpants bunched at his ankles, grasping at her breasts like the horn of a bucking bronco's saddle and flossing his teeth with her pubic hair. Greg had a disappointing mouth. Meg suspected he didn't possess the tongue strength to eat an ice cream cone without calamitous dripping.

Hot action on your phone there? Sara plucks the lime wedge from her glass, tongues it into her mouth and chomps at it like a cow.

School work, Meg says and tucks her phone away.

Sara focuses her eyes down her straw's tunnel. Mom still drinking?

Meg nods. She's tried everything. It's a part of her.

People quit things.

Maybe if I had some backup.

I wasn't going to stay away forever.

Nineteen years?

You never looked for me.

You didn't want to be found.

You know I did, Meg.

I guess we were all playing games.

I did call Mom.

She told me. When you were pregnant.

She never asked me to come back.

Maybe she wanted you to want to come home.

What she always said about Dad.

Meg floods her throat with whisky to untangle her stomach. She tells Sara she wasn't old enough to name him when he left.

To Meg, he is *my father*, never *Dad*. She and Sara have not struggled in tandem. Sara misses her dad. Meg misses an idea, a man she cannot locate in herself. A man who only wanted her when he thought she was someone else.

Glad you got in touch now, Sara says.

Of course.

Meg looks away from Sara, that accumulating lint ball of everything that is wrong with her family. Her father's inclination to run, her mother's inclination to blame. Meg scans the bar for a potential celebration-of-life date. A server with painfully manageable straight red hair and a mandala tattoo peeking out from under her hot pants do-si-dos round bar tables with a tray full of wildly strawed drinks. She wears Chinatown discount bin flip-flops that Meg immediately covets. Why does Meg try so hard with her four-hundred-dollar clogs? She hates and admires this woman. She either wants to fuck her or be her, she never knows which. The server hands a bottle of Blue Buck to a kid in his twenties, man-bunned golden hair, ripped jeans pasted to his thighs exposing slick knees, his back curled and face flitting like an eel to catch his reflection in every female's eye. Meg is four Italian Country Singers into the night, but she is sure this is the ghost of her father here to tell her she doesn't need a date, she has him.

I think that's him, Meg says.

Sara turns toward the golden boy. What are you... who?

Our father. His ghost.

You think he's really dead?

Meg laughs into Sara's chest. If he's not dead why is his ghost right there?

You're drunk, Meg.

We need to bring him to the celebration of life. Meg stands up, steadies herself.

Meg, sit down. Forget it.

He wants his foot back.

Sit down, Meg. Sara slaps a hand to Meg's stool, then softens. Thought you might be happy to see me.

Meg pokes her pointer finger into Sara's shoulder. Thought *you* might apologize for taking off on me.

Only living my life, Meg.

Glad one of us gets to.

Sara lifts, then slams her empty glass to the bar. Oh, poor Meg, she says. Going to fancy bars and women's feminist school.

It's called gender studies.

I don't even have a fucking job.

Well I have about fifty. Fuck you, Sara. I've been literally wiping the drool from Mom's chin my whole life.

Literally? I've never seen you do that.

Too busy chasing your dad.

Not my fault he loved me more.

Meg closes her mouth. Breathes in. *He didn't care.* Breathes out. *So why do you?* Meg breathes in. She holds herself back from mounting Sara like a shrieking bat demon, ripping every hair from her audacious scalp, eating her face and spitting it into the cavities where her soul should be. Meg wants to scream at Sara that she's the one who found their father. She's the one he crossed an ocean to be with and Sara's the one he crossed an ocean to leave. Meg's the one he pursued, the one he wanted. But even in her drunken state Meg knows revealing this will lead to a line of questioning that would only prove the opposite.

Meg pushes off from the bar and staggers toward the ghost of her father. He sits on a stool, his toes perched on its stretcher like talons, legs triangular. He cradles one hand in the other as though nursing a slowly suffocating minnow. Meg's stomach relaxes. But it's nonsensical to feel safe in a man's effeminacy—it is not the brawn of a man that will destroy her. She stops in front of him and places her hand where the minnow would be.

Would you like to join me at your funeral? she says.

The ghost jerks his head back a few inches. What?

You look like my father.

He cups an ear and leans toward her. Sorry?

Come outside, Meg says, and he understands. He holds her hand and guides her out the door of the bar.

Let's go, she says once outside. Do you have a car or anything?

Her father's ghost points toward a fixed-gear bicycle chained to a post. My wheels, he says.

Of course.

Meg bodychecks him to the brick wall of the bar. She kisses him hard, smears her wet mouth all over that asshole's face with her eye on Sara's profile—stuck to her stool, lips drawn around her straw while Meg's father chooses her. He turns and pushes her against the cold brick. The December air is a frigid hand rubbing salt into her pores. Her father's ghost traces a thumb from her hip down the crease of her thigh. The wind off the ocean blows up her skirt and she feels exposed to the waist, like a wave has crested between her thighs. His thumb is inside her now, here on the street. Men whose hair has never seen scissors, who are forever cloaked in the reek of sweat and piss push their lives, teetering under tarps in shopping carts, past them.

Hey, Meg says. Her father slides his hand out from her skirt. Hey, she says again. He looks up, looks her in the eyes. His hands around Meg's waist now, she teeters between them on her clogs. She holds his gaze for an uncomfortably long time, arms crossed at her chest against the cold, embracing something invisible.

Sara's not sure her mother has changed these sheets since she left home at eighteen. Last night, when she came home from the bar, Sara lifted the covers and released a pocket of her teenaged self. Patchouli, Orange Crush Lip Smacker and scalp grease. Courtney Love still looks down from her wall, doll eyes and sea-star pout wobbling the tightrope of victimhood and smug fame. A forgiving person, a person like Nik, would see this bedroom as a shrine, a sign of hope for her return. Sara sees it as laziness, a quarantine of her existence.

She lifts an arm above her head and fingers the Braille heart she poked into her wall with a thumbtack that week in middle school when she thought she loved the boy who boned her in a closet. She didn't love him, she loved his Pixies T-shirt, his toadstool hair and the electric rush up her throat when he addressed her by name after ignoring her for days. Being in this room brings back an angry loneliness. Mom took care of Meg, but even at six years old Sara spackled her own Wonder Bread walls with apricot jam.

At home, in Edmonton, she huffs infantile resentment toward Nik, she grasps at power that is hers to hold, but too scattered to collect. Sara's daughter is almost the age she was when she left home. When Juni was little, she and Sara were friends, twins. Nik held firm the scaffolding within which they played. Now, Juniper is fourteen years old and Sara can't bear to be her mother. Once the first fat deposits accumulated around the outskirts of her nipples, Juni's worship turned to resentment, bordering on hatred. Their shared exploits became tedious wastes of Juniper's time, which was suddenly spent worshipping all that Sara despised: the blood of sentient beings, boys outfitted in *Thrasher* hoodies and other lame relics of the nineties, YouTube makeup tutorials. Sara knows Juniper wants to become anything but her. Does she remember the closeness they shared when she was a child the way Sara remembers her time with Dad? Maybe she would if Sara had truly disappeared like he did, in body and spirit. Sara's phone rings. It's Nik.

You noticed I'm gone.

You're in Victoria?

Thanks for your condolences.

Should I bother asking why you took off without telling me?

My sister found me on Facebook. I'm here for the funeral. Celebration of life. Whatever.

You have shit here, Sara. A daughter.

She loves you more.

I'm around more.

Right. You're at the coffee shop with your favourite barista.

I don't play favourites. Nik teases Sara like they're kids playing at jealousy. Like he's not an unemployed forty-year-old man planting himself among twenty-five-year-old girls to inflate his used-condom ego.

Sara hangs up to prevent the destruction of this thing, whatever it is they have. This stretched-out bungee cord with which she hooks herself to the world.

He calls back five minutes later because, God knows why, he depends on this too.

You know me, Nik says. Every awful thing. But they don't.

Sara reaches up and traces the punctured heart on her wall with a fingertip. I get it, she says. That doesn't make it okay.

I do love you.

Remember when you'd say that without the *do*?

I would've come if you asked me. And Juniper.

You want her to meet her grandfather's severed foot?

You need to stop disappearing.

You too, Nik.

Touché, he says. He exhales loud and slow into the phone. I'm sorry.

Sara's mother knocks at the door and doesn't even jiggle the knob. A throwback to Sara's border-patrol teenaged years.

I do love you, Sara says. I love you. And she hangs up. She opens the door to her mother, a serving tray against her waist stacked with two cups of tea, cream, sugar and a plate of bulk-bin convenience store cookies. The kind that taste like sweet talcum powder and are sticky in the wrong places. There are parts of her mother that haven't changed—her stubbled shins, those faded grey sweatpants that must be made of the strongest polyester fibres known to humankind—but then there's her rainbow hair, gradations of purple from root to tip, frizzy and fluffed around her face like cotton candy. It used to hang, toasty brown, brush her cheeks and flip at her shoulders. And the tray. Servitude and its accessories have never been a part of her skill set.

She rests the tray on Sara's dresser and asks, Sugar?

Please. And a moistened towelette.

Hmm? Sara's mother places hands to hips and surveys the room. I kept it just the way you left it.

Were you afraid of me when I lived here?

You didn't scare me. Sara's mother looks to the ceiling. Maybe a bit.

Were you relieved when I left?

Yes and no. Mostly yes. She looks at Sara head-on as she nods. There are some things Sara couldn't appreciate about her mother until she became a mother herself. Her thoughtless honesty Sara took for unkindness. Her vulnerability she took for weakness.

It's nice to have you here, her mother says. I get lonely.

Meg clomps into the apartment and peeks around Sara's door, cautious and guilty. She's bedizened in a black potato-sack dress cinched at the waist with a hot-pink skull-and-crossbones scarf. Attached to her hand is a little boy, mango-cheeked with cotton balls of blond hair. He's in black pants and an orange T-shirt: *Beacon Hill Children's Farm Volunteer*.

I didn't know, Meg says, dress for a funeral or celebration?

I'm dressed like Halloween, says the boy. Cause there's skeletons and ghosts.

Smart thinking. I'm your Auntie Sara. Sara extends an arm to the boy.

My name is Sebastian and I'm eight years old.

Sara shakes Sebastian's hand and looks at Meg. Last night at the bar, Sara said something unforgivable to her, beyond apologies. An insult siblings from normal families toss back and forth at each other. A harmless weapon, like a couch cushion. The temporary hoarding of what is in ample supply. Sara claimed her father's love as hers alone and it was unforgivable because it was true. She watched Meg fall apart over a golden impression of their father. When he walked away from her, Sara went outside and held Meg tight to the bricks, squeezed her, small and wobbly like a clogged child playing dress-up, until the glue set. Meg made a sponge of Sara's sweater. Does she have to quilt herself back together on all the other nights when Sara's not there?

This look is very punk rock, Sara says, and tugs at Meg's scarf. Meg doesn't look at her, but she brushes her fingers against Sara's and tugs at her scarf too, and Sara knows they're okay.

Ricky looks like a pot-bellied ten-year-old boy with laugh lines and leathered skin but Donny could stand in for Keith Richards. Like his lushness was vacuumed out through his asshole. He extends a knobby, heavily metalled hand to Gwen and she shakes it. Long time, he says. That's what everyone at Damian's funeral is saying, even those she's never met. Men in need of a belt and a dollop of shampoo and women with sun-weary skin expelled in all directions from leather halters hover in clumps around fingers of celery, puddles of ranch dip, cheese cubes impaled on tooth-pick stakes and rounds of flesh rolled into themselves like tented cub scouts. What was Meg thinking? Cold cuts at a funeral? It brings to mind the grey lumps of pulled-pork tissue Gwen imagines bulged from Damian's ankle, bobbing at the shore-line. Gwen's not sure why Meg's blown up an old photo of Iggy onstage at the Commodore, either.

Shepps here? Donny says.

Gwen points to the poppy-flanked stage where Shepps is set-ting up equipment for the reunion of Dorothy's Rainbow.

Donny steps up and yanks at the cables Shepps is fiddling with. I'll do lead vocals and guitar tonight, Donny says.

I rehearsed vocals and guitar, says Shepps. You don't even play guitar.

Bass is a guitar.

Missing two strings.

Donny scoffs at this. I was in Fitz of Depression. A real band. In Olympia.

What's that supposed to mean?

You could blow into a gourd and call yourself a band in Olympia.

We played with Bikini Kill.

Did you sing and play guitar?

I played bass.

My point.

You're on lead bass tonight, Shepps. All you ever wanted.

Gwen can't believe they're fighting like they did when this band mattered. This is one show. At a funeral. Yet here she is listening in the shadows like she did in her twenties.

Gwen wanders to the refreshments, stacked precariously on some old lady's bridge table Meg found in the storage closet dressed with a plastic-coated, flamboyantly flowered cloth. Gwen ladles out a cup of punch and hides around the corner to top it up. A saggy man with receding grey-white bedhead stumbles by with a sleeping bag in tow, its drawstring hooked to his crusty index finger. A radius of decay—human skin marinated in curdled milk, sweaty socks, watermelon left on a hot sidewalk—wafts arounds him. He noses interest in the contents of Gwen's bag like a cartoon dog at a steaming pie. Gwen pulls out her flask, which is full of apple cider vinegar. Even Shepps thinks it's vodka. But Gwen is sober. Mostly sober. The vinegar gives her that warm burn, fools her body into believing she'll soon feel at home. This way, she keeps them all barely out of reach—not gone, but not hers. Floating in the maybe. How easy it is to fool when you require others to cling to the status quo.

Spare a little? says the man.

You a friend of Damian's?

Sailed to China with him in a shipping container.

He'd rather be hot-boxed with the foulest reek of humanity than share a bed with me.

Whoever heard of a dry funeral? he says.

I got you, says Gwen. She retrieves her backup mickey of vodka and hands it to the man.

The man takes a drink. Wouldn't take it personal, he says. Dams was scared of standing still the way we're scared of jumping.

Throughout the thirty-eight years since Gwen entangled herself with him, people have shared with her their versions of Damian. He'd tell them one secret and they thought they'd figured him out. But he didn't even know himself. Most people stitch themselves into a stuff sack that is moulded by the perceptions and desires of others. Damian avoided the sack, anything definite, binding. An eternal question.

Problem is, Gwen says, that made him a giant asshole.

The man laughs a hearty gurgling guffaw. We all die alone, eh?

Gwen swipes her bottle of vodka from the man, takes a long, three-gulp swig and hands it back. Keep it, Gwen says. I'm sober. Starting now.

The man saunters off and is replaced by Meg, shuffling staccato in her clogs like an Irish dancer. She squeezes Gwen at the shoulders.

I wasn't drinking, Gwen says.

Mom. Mom, no one's eating the meat and we're out of celery. And I can't find Donny.

They'll eat the meat when there's nothing else left.

How long does meat last at room temperature?

Who cares? We don't know these creeps.

Meg leans against the wall and slides to the floor, cross-legged. This was a stupid idea, she says.

Gwen squats beside Meg. They both look out into the hall at the band of misfits Meg has gathered, each one orbiting themselves, attempting to gather the others into their sphere of influence. Sara and Sebastian stand in the centre of this galaxy of sociopaths, holding hands and wiggling their bums to the background music Meg has chosen: early punk mixed with wistful new age.

This is great, Meggie, Gwen says. Did you know your father sailed to China with the smelliest man on earth?

Meg laughs. Beats hanging out with us.

You're a better person than me, Meg. All this for a man who deserted you.

What would my father do if he were here?

He'd eat all that meat.

Would he like this?

He would die to be here, Meg.

Mom.

Give a foot to be here.

Seriously. Meg buries a wet face into Gwen's shoulder. Gwen hopes it's wet from tears and not snot, but she doesn't say anything.

I'll find Shepps, Gwen says. He'll sort out the band.

Gwen knows exactly where to find Shepps. Crying in the men's room, farthest stall from the door. She storms in and tells the men at the urinals she's seen a penis before, what makes theirs so special?

She extends a hand under the stall door. You good, Shepps?

Two sneakered feet lower from the toilet seat to the floor and Shepps' hands cradle Gwen's.

Thinking about the early days, he says. When we'd play shows at halls like this.

All ages, someone's mom's cookies for sale at the door.

What happened?

Everyone grew up, Shepps.

Donny owns a Toyota dealership in Coeur d'Alene.

Sellout. Where's he at?

In the parking lot getting his tarot read by one of Dams' old girlfriends.

She sounds lame.

Can't beat the original.

Gwen smacks one of Shepps' sneakers.

Okay, Shepps says. Let's show these punks what's what.

The hum and crackle of a guitar plugging into its amp triggers an instinctual jealous heating of Gwen's blood. She swallows it back. Her life no longer depends on this. Meg steps up to the mic in front of Donny, his guitar cinched waist-high like Buddy Holly, Shepps to his left, bass strung low and dejected, and Ricky stoned and oblivious at the drums.

Thank you for joining us tonight to celebrate our father, husband, bandmate and friend: Damian Costello.

Meg enunciates Damian's name with a level of fanfare not reciprocated by the crowd, who now graze like flies at the remaining bits of meat. She curls herself over the mic again.

Thank you for finishing off the meat. I wasn't sure about it.

Meg clears her throat.

Um, anyway, thirty-one years ago today, on December 13, 1990, Dorothy's Rainbow played their last gig. And tonight, in honour of my father, we have a very special reunion performance. Let's give it up for the almost-all-original lineup of arguably the best punk band to come out of Victoria, British Columbia: Dorothy's Rainbow.

Meg claps, Sara whoops and Gwen draws out a loud *woo*. The crowd licks nitrates from their fingertips.

Donny grabs the mic. This is our version of "God Save the Queen." When we first got together, it was "God Save Pierre Elliott Trudeau," and here we are singing "God Save Justin." Makes a guy feel real fucking old.

Donny draws a laugh from the crowd, but he cannot play guitar. Or sing. And it's clear he hasn't remembered the lyrics from rehearsal the day before. *God save Justine, He's so fucking mean. He made you a moron, selling out for a pipeline.* Doesn't rhyme, doesn't even have rhythm. He sounds like a slam poet, ranting into the mic while he grates across his fretboard with a pic. The crowd smiles politely, heads drifting toward the now-empty refreshment table and back to the stage. Shepps' eyes are desperate, the way they were when Gwen would respond to his proclamations of love with a wide-eyed nod and maybe a yank at his balls for distraction.

This is their last chance. She could let this bullshit happen and go to bed tonight and sleep and wake up again and again or she could get up there and send off the man who's haunted her entire fucking adult life. Scream out the *whys*, *wheres*, *with whos* that have plagued her for thirty-one years. She gulps a swig of pure apple cider vinegar. Feels the burn. Shakes her body. Scissors a leg onto the stage. Shepps' eyes soften. *This is for you and me, Shepps.* Gwen takes the mic while Donny solos like a bass player, picking methodically at one string at a time.

Hold up, hold up, Gwen says. We're doing this right. Donny, you're on bass. Shepps, you take guitar. I'll sing. I am punk rock.

Shepps and Donny switch instruments with the agape faces Sara and Meg would wear when Gwen yelled at them for not noticing her bang trim or for singing along to Alanis Morissette on the radio. Meg and Sara clap, arms above their heads, together. Meg's forehead is free of the lines that appear when all is not going according to plan. Her eyes are mellow, without their usual swift, avian focus. Sebastian grips the edge of the stage, hops from toe to toe and wobbles his head with the unselfconscious plasticity of a child.

Gwen wraps two hands around the mic like she's strangling a lover, props her left leg up on the monitor. Black Mary Janes, sagging white knee socks to cover her unshaven December calves, a fifty-nine-year-old schoolgirl. She clears her throat, looks to Shepps to be sure he's ready.

Let's rock it better than he ever could, she shouts into the mic. This one's called "Raccoon Massacre." Two, three, four. Sexy little bandits, Flo-Jo fingernails… The lyrics surface from Gwen's body memory. If she tries to conjure them, she'll forget, like a dream. Gwen has wished Damian dead more times than she can count. Now that it's happened, she has at least one answer. Everything else can float away. Damian must be so pleased, immersed timelessly in unstill waters. An eternal question.

Notes

This work was created with the help of the Canada Council for the Arts. Earlier versions of some of these chapters have been published in the following: "Poseurs" in *Numéro Cinq* and *Coming Attractions 16*, "Sock Daddy" in *Southwest Review*, "Popular Girls" in *Grain*, "The Postcard" (as "Dad, Offstage") in *The New Quarterly*, "Room and Board" in *Prairie Fire* and *Coming Attractions 16*, "Big Spoon" in *The Puritan*, "Angling" in *filling Station* and *Coming Attractions 16*, "What is Good" in *Cosmonauts Avenue*, "Tom's Wedding" in *the moth: art and literature*, "The Rest of Him" in *Event* and *The Journey Prize Stories 32*, and "After Gwen" in *The Minola Review*.

Acknowledgements

S ince this is my first book, I'll begin by thanking Pearl Luke, who told me I was a writer before I believed it myself. Without that encouragement, I may not have carried on scribbling while my babies napped. I am grateful to the Victoria Writers' Society, especially Dave and Debra Henry, who were my first community of writers. Acting as VWS secretary gave me purpose during a very dark time.

Next, thanks to John Barton and Rhonda Batchelor for taking a chance and inviting me into the *Malahat Review*. I don't think this book would exist had I not spent those five years bunny watching with you in the Clearihue building. I learned so much from listening in on selection meetings, office gossip, and most of all by being introduced to brilliant writers both on the page and off, many of whom have become dear friends. Above all, Garth Martens, Kyeren Regehr, Eliza Robertson, Rich Cole, Benjamin Willems and Zoey Leigh Peterson—who has helped me in countless ways, but most of all by going through the majority of the chapters in this book with the amount of care and thoughtfulness that she affords her friendships.

The Elite Eight at the Banff Centre, led by Alexander MacLeod, were a huge help and boost of confidence. Special thanks to Alex for providing me with the last line for "Room and Board" and to Jon Shanahan, Kira Proctor and Paige Cooper (a.k.a. The Night Ladies) for being weird and wonderful friends as well as readers for many more of these chapters.

Many thanks also to Alan Warner, who sent me my first and favourite piece of fan mail, for being a supportive and hilarious correspondent, and for your work, which is an inspiration. Thank you also to Douglas Glover and Mark Anthony Jarman for being early supporters and publishers of my work as well as for your brilliant contributions to Canadian literature. I'd like to thank every magazine that published chapters from this book—above all, *The New Quarterly*, who gave me my first real publication and consequently led me to believe I might be able to write a whole book. I am so thrilled and grateful to the 2020 Journey Prize jury for choosing "The Rest of Him" to be included in the anthology, which has been a dream of mine since I became aware of it—as well as to *Event* and to the other magazines who've sent my work to be considered for the prize this year and in years past. Eternal gratitude to Silas White for seeing something publishable in this book.

My most effusive thanks to LORNA JACKSON!!!!! who took me on as her grad student and pushed me through many, many edits of most of these chapters during my MFA at the University of Victoria. Lorna, you are brilliant and I wish everything I write could pass muster with you before going out into the world. Thank you also to those who helped me shape these chapters while at UVic: Lee Henderson, Bill Gaston, Sam Shelstad, Michael LaPointe, Robbie Huebner, K'ari Fisher, Stephanie Harrington, Annabel Howard and Kelsey Lauder.

Like most writers, I am not in this for the money and am therefore grateful to the Canada Council for the Arts, which not only supports Canadian magazines and publishers, but the writers who appear on their pages. Thank you for affording me the time, post-graduation, to finish this book before I surrendered my body and soul to minimum-wage work. And thank you to my co-workers at the Greater Victoria Public Library (especially Perry, Wendy, Aaron, Derek, Matt B. and Martin) for making that hamster wheel infinitely more fun to tread. On a slightly embarrassing note, since I'm technically too old to qualify as a millennial, I'd like to thank my parents for funding my MFA. It'll pay off one day, I swear.

I'm indebted to many sources, notably: *Drunk Mom* by Jowita Bydlowska; *Touching from a Distance: Ian Curtis and Joy Division* by Deborah Curtis; *All Your Ears Can Hear: Underground Music in Victoria, BC 1978–1984*; and Paulina Ortlieb's documentary *Somewhere to Go: Punk Victoria* were all helpful in writing this book.

Most importantly of all, I thank my writing group: K'ari, Steph, Annabel and Erin Frances Fisher, not only for your professional critique and support for this novel, but for your friendship and emotional support. All of you astound me with your intelligence, talent, strength and dance moves. I cannot imagine my life without you.

Finally, I thank my three boys who have helped me to be efficient with the small amounts of free time they offer me, who fill my life with meaning and unconditional love, and who give me faith that the next generation of men will be respectful, emotionally honest, beautiful people. I am so proud of you. And, though it is dedicated to you, don't actually read this book.

PHOTO BY ALEXANDRA STEPHANSON

Susan Sanford Blades lives in Victoria, BC, where she completed an MFA in creative writing at the University of Victoria. She has been published in the anthologies *The Journey Prize Stories 32: The Best of Canada's New Writers* and *Coming Attractions 16*, and in literary magazines across Canada as well as in the US and Ireland, including *Minola Review, Event, the moth, The Puritan, Numéro Cinq, The New Quarterly, Grain* and *Prairie Fire*.